Adrift in
CHESHIRE BAY

USA TODAY BESTSELLING AUTHOR
H.M. SHANDER

Adrift in Cheshire Bay

Published by H.M. Shander Publishing
Copyright 2021 H.M. Shander

Cover Design: Eleanor Lloyd-Jones @ Shower of Schmidt Designs
Editing: PWA & IDIM Editorial
Shander, H.M., 1975—Adrift in Cheshire Bay

Dedicated to a summer of broken dreams,
afternoons spent in the backyard
under the red umbrella with an iced coffee in hand.
And to the Squirrels — Duncan & Carlos and their kids,
Cedar, George & Rusty

Table of Contents

Chapter One

I clicked off the walkie-talkie and walked to the bank of full-length windows, my shoes echoing across the waxed tile floor. Flight 145 inbound from Seattle was just beginning its descent. The Cessna 140 bobbed lightly in the breeze, its wings slicing the crisp September air as it coasted over the tree line.

Off to the side, working the tarmac like he owned it, was the love of my life—Mitch Macomber. Airport mechanic, baggage handler, and walking, talking ad for grease-stained sex appeal. Even from this distance, I could smell the faint trace of orange wipes and jet fuel, a scent I'd come to associate with both home and desire.

Some women say they could never work with their boyfriends, but I couldn't imagine *not*. We drove in together each morning, sharing a thermos of coffee and a Spotify playlist that was mostly his, then went our separate ways—he to the garage, me to the front desk as the face of West Coast Air and Cheshire Bay Airport. We crossed paths during the day, exchanged smirks, maybe a quick kiss behind the hangar, then clocked out and went back to our house in the center of our tiny village. Predictable. Perfect.

"Flight 145 has touched down," Mitch's voice crackled over the walkie.

"Check," I said, and smiled.

Cheshire Bay usually got two flights a day—sometimes three in peak season—and that was considered busy. Most were intra-island, little puddle-jumper hops between towns tucked into the coastline. But a few times a week, we got a mainland arrival from Vancouver or Seattle. The Seattle ones were my favorite. They brought in people who seemed… different. Curious. Open.

This was the last flight of the day, which meant tonight was reserved for something far more exciting: dinner with Mitch. Five years. I'd somehow managed to keep a relationship alive for five whole years, and tonight we were celebrating at The Harbour Chophouse—fancy table, ocean view, cloth napkins, the whole deal. September was still tourist-heavy, but the restaurant saved ten percent of its seating for locals. Tonight, we were one of the lucky few.

Outside, Mitch moved toward the plane with the lazy confidence of a man who knew engines better than people. His coveralls hung loose over his lean frame as he opened the luggage hatch and gently unloaded the bags onto the tarmac.

I turned my gaze toward the plane door, drumming my fingers on the window frame in a rhythm that matched my pulse. I loved meeting the passengers— loved being the first face to greet them, to answer their questions, point them to motels, trails, restaurants, or hidden beaches. I took pride in knowing every shortcut and secret spot between Cheshire Bay and the next two towns over. If they had questions, I had answers.

The door opened, and the first passenger stepped out—a silver-haired gentleman in a worn fishing hat, leaning heavily on a cane.

I opened the glass door and stepped into the salty air, offering him a warm smile and a chilled bottle of water.

"Good afternoon, and welcome to Cheshire Bay," I said, holding out the bottle.

He tipped his hat politely and waved off the water. "No thank you, miss. Flight was smooth."

I could tell from his coloring that Eric—our best pilot and my closest friend—had given them a turbulence-free ride.

"Glad to hear it. Do you have a ride picking you up, or would you like me to call someone?"

"Oh, Julia's got me covered." He pointed behind me to a young woman stepping into the terminal. "That's my granddaughter. D'ya know her?"

I grinned. "No, sir, I don't. But I'm glad you made it safe. Enjoy your stay."

Next came a woman and her young son, the boy tugging at a suitcase that kept listing to one side. His small hands fumbled with the handle while the woman held tightly to his wrist, her expression tight and unreadable.

I stepped forward. "Can I help with that?" I crouched slightly so the boy wouldn't feel talked over. "I can carry your suitcase, if you'd like."

"No." The woman's voice had a sharp edge. Then, a pause, followed by a weighty sigh. "Fine. Thank you."

I gave the boy a soft smile. "How about we make a trade? I'll take the suitcase, and you take this bottle of water."

He looked up at his mom for permission, then released the bag with relief and clutched the cold bottle like a treasure.

I pulled the handle and hoisted the case with ease.

"Uneventful flight?" I asked the woman, keeping my tone light.

She smelled expensive—something floral and classic, like Chanel No. 5 and wore a fitted cream blouse with the kind of creases that only come from sitting still and tightly composed.

"Uneventful, which is always a plus," she replied

without looking at me.

We entered the terminal, and I scanned the area for Mitch or Eric. Eric was doing a walkaround, checking for forgotten items like he always did. Mitch was beneath the plane, doing his usual post-flight inspection. Eric trusted Mitch implicitly, and so did I.

The pilot descended the stairs holding up a white teddy bear. "Someone forget a friend?"

The boy's eyes lit up, but his mother's brow pinched.

"Jackson, how many times do I have to remind you? Keep track of your things!"

Jackson hung his head. Eric crouched beside him and waved the bear gently.

"What's his name?" Eric asked, all kindness.

"Mr. Fluffy," the boy mumbled.

"Well, Mr. Fluffy had a great time flying today, but I think he'd rather stick close to his buddy." Eric handed it over, and Jackson hugged it fiercely.

Eric gave me a wink and walked to the desk to log his report.

I turned to the mother. "Do you have someone picking you up? I can call one of the local taxis if you need."

She hesitated. Her eyes flicked around the room like she wasn't sure whether to speak or bolt. Then, with a breath, she said, "Actually... I'm looking for Mitch

Macomber. I heard he works here."

The name landed in my ears like a firecracker in a quiet room.

I blinked. "Yes, I—yes. I know Mitch."

Eric's pen stilled on the clipboard. He looked up sharply, brows furrowed.

The woman's shoulders eased. "Thank God." Her voice dropped to a whisper. "Is there a way I could contact him? A number, maybe?"

"I'm afraid I can't give out employee contact info," I said, trying to keep my tone neutral. "But I'd be happy to take your number and pass it along."

Her eyes scanned the space again, more urgently now. "Does he work *here*, here? Like, *now*?"

Before I could answer, the door opened with a faint whoosh, and Mitch strolled in, wiping his hands on an orange shop towel that smelled like citrus and motor oil. My chest did a little flutter—until the woman gasped.

"Mitchy?"

Mitchy?

Mitch stopped cold. His six-two frame straightened, and his eyes went wide. "Jas?"

The woman walked straight toward him, auburn hair swinging behind her like a cape. She threw her arms around him in a hug so fast, it even startled her son.

I instinctively took a step back.

Beside me, Eric stood taller. He didn't speak, but

his posture changed, alert and ready.

"Oh. My. God." Her voice cracked with joy. "How are you?"

Mitch disengaged from the hug with a stunned laugh that didn't sound quite right. "Wow. Hey. Jasmine. This is... unexpected."

She smoothed her blouse and stood proudly beside her boy.

"It's been a while, right?" she said.

"Yeah." Mitch's voice was rough around the edges. His eyes flicked toward me—just for a second— but it was enough.

Jasmine looked at her son, who was now flying Mr. Fluffy across the couch, his legs swinging in loose rhythm.

"I thought it was time for you two to meet," she said gently.

Mitch stared at the boy.

I forgot how to breathe.

Jasmine's voice dropped, but it still carried. "He's yours. That's your son."

I didn't realize I'd reached for Eric's arm until my fingers gripped tight around his sleeve.

Mitch's mouth opened, then closed. His gaze stayed fixed on the child as the orange towel in his hand slowly dropped to the floor.

Inside my chest, my heart skipped a beat, then

another.

Then it slammed so hard against my ribs I could have sworn the whole room heard it.

Chapter Two

ric's arm shot out just in time to steady me, his hand pressing firmly against my back before I could collapse. My knees had gone hollow, the floor felt impossibly far away, and all I could think was *no, not now*.

This morning—just this morning—I'd stood in our tiny bathroom, barefoot and shaking, holding a plastic stick that promised everything was about to change.

I was pregnant.

And I had planned to tell Mitch tonight. Over dinner. Our five-year anniversary. A table by the window, ocean view, candlelight, cloth napkins. I'd imagined the smile on his face. The tears, maybe. The joy.

But now?

Now I couldn't even move.

Mitch was motionless. He hadn't blinked. Hadn't spoken. Hadn't looked at me since she said *that* word.

Son.

I nudged Eric's arm in thanks but still couldn't make my legs work. I stared at the boy—Jackson—and tried to see it. Tried to find some glimmer of resemblance. The hair, maybe, in color or curl. But the face? All Jasmine. The soft curve of his jaw, the shape of his eyes.

And the accent. American.

Mitch was Canadian through and through.

It didn't make sense.

Couldn't make sense.

It had to be a mistake.

A misunderstanding.

"Why don't you come over and say hi to Jackson, Mitchy?" Jasmine coaxed, her voice light, as if she hadn't just detonated a bomb in the middle of our lives.

Mitch blinked at last, slowly, and turned his head toward his alleged son. His Adam's apple bobbed violently as he swallowed. "Uh… hey there, little guy."

But his eyes didn't linger on the child. Just for a flicker, a heartbeat, they found mine. And in them, I saw it: fear. Raw and unfiltered. Not shock. Not confusion.

Fear.

Like he already knew.

Eric stepped into the heavy silence. "Why don't you all sit down for a minute," he said, calm as ever, motioning toward the waiting area. A couch and a couple of worn, angular chairs sat untouched, more decoration than function. Jackson was already giving them more use than they'd seen in months, toy cars spinning across the scuffed linoleum.

I backed up until I could feel the edge of the reception desk against my spine. It anchored me. Sort of. My brain was screaming and spinning all at once. Mitch. My Mitch. He had a kid? With *her*? And I was the one... I was supposed to tell him about *our* baby tonight.

I pressed a hand over my belly and felt... nothing. Too early for movement. Too soon for proof. But the ache inside me throbbed like a second heartbeat.

Across the room, Mitch sat stiffly on the arm of a chair, his hands dangling uselessly between his knees. Jasmine plopped into a seat like she owned the place. Jackson didn't seem to notice the tension; he was already back to zooming his cars, lost in a world of his own.

"I know I'm just... dropping this whole situation on you," Jasmine said with a hint of fake remorse, "but I need you to sign a few documents urgently."

Her words were practiced. Like she'd rehearsed them. Like this wasn't even hard for her. Mitch, on the other hand, looked like he was about to pass out. Still pale. Still rigid. Still no expression. The kind of stillness that comes only from total disorientation.

"Eric," I said, my voice breaking against the jagged edge of my breath.

He was back behind the desk, scribbling something on a flight report, but looked up immediately. "Yeah?"

"Is he... okay?" I didn't dare speak louder. I didn't trust my voice.

Eric's gaze darted to Mitch. His jaw tightened. "I think it's... a lot. But yeah. He'll be okay."

"He doesn't *look* okay."

"Well, his whole life just flipped inside out." Eric tapped the pen against the counter, thinking. "Imagine what that'd do to you."

I didn't have to imagine.

It had already happened.

At 6:46 a.m. today, to be exact. The second line had appeared on the test. Faint but unmistakable. I'd driven all the way to the next town to buy it—no way I could risk getting caught at our local drugstore. In Cheshire Bay, secrets didn't last long. Hell, they didn't even get to *be* secrets. Not for long. Just ask Lily.

"How's Lily?" I asked, needing a new topic, a safer place to land.

Eric softened. "She's good. Tired. She slept most of yesterday."

"She's due any day now, right?"

"Yup. We're ready." He smiled gently. "Any day."

"You're going to be a great dad."

"Thanks." He gave me a look. "I plan to be." Then he closed his binder, tucked it into the shelf, and sighed. "Alright. Heading out."

But he didn't move. He stood still, looking at Mitch.

"I'll check on him first."

He made his way over to the seating area, boots thudding against the concrete floor.

"Jasmine, right?"

She nodded, rifling through her purse like she had somewhere more important to be.

"Look, obviously this is... big. You dropping this on Mitch? It's a lot. Maybe give him a day to take it in. Leave your number or the place you're staying. He'll reach out."

"We've rented a cabin on Bay Drive. Near the end," she said, flipping through some printed reservation papers. She held one up.

Eric snapped a picture with his phone. "Appreciate it. Just... give him time."

She nodded with tight lips. "We're only here for a week, and I really do need his signature on those documents." She patted her bag for good measure before turning to Jackson, who was crawling under the chair now. "Time to pack up, baby."

And like that, the storm gathered its things.

But I was still in uniform. Still the representative

of West Coast Air. Even if my personal world had cracked wide open, I had a job to do.

Swallowing hard, I stepped forward. "Do you need a ride?"

She held up her phone. "My cousin's already on the way."

She tugged Jackson up by the hand, and just as they reached the door, she turned back.

"Oh—his suitcase. Do you mind grabbing it? I'm sorry, I'm just—"

I shook my head before she could finish. "Not at all." I walked past Mitch and forced a soft touch to his leg. "Hey, honey," I whispered.

Nothing. No reaction.

He didn't even blink.

My throat burned, but I grabbed the small suitcase and hurried it to the door.

"You have a great day," I said automatically, voice dull and empty.

What I *wanted* to say was: *How dare you.*

What I *wanted* to do was scream. Or cry. Or crawl into bed and vanish for a week.

But I couldn't.

Not yet.

When they were gone, I returned to the building and sat next to Mitch. He still hadn't moved.

Eric came back around. "Take him home," he

said, already grabbing my walkie-talkie. "We're done for the day."

I gathered our things slowly, carefully, like it might help stitch the world back together.

Eric gave me a solid pat between the shoulders as I helped Mitch stand and guided him toward the car.

He was dead weight. Barely functioning.

I opened the passenger side and helped him in. Then I climbed behind the wheel.

"Say hi to Lily for me," I called to Eric through the door.

"I'll have her call you later. I'll swing by too. Just to check in."

"Thanks," I said, and turned the key.

As we pulled away, Mitch spoke for the first time in ten minutes.

"After all this time... she shows up now?" His voice was distant. Paper thin.

I looked at him. "Should I cancel our reservation?"

Even the idea of calling the restaurant made my heart twist. I'd imagined this night for so long.

"I don't know," Mitch said, still staring out the window. "I just need to think."

I watched the trees blur past as we drove wondering how long I needed to wait to tell him. One day? Two?

He clearly hadn't planned on fatherhood, not now. Maybe not ever. That much was written all over his face.

So when *should* I tell him?

How long is too long to hold your own life back for someone else's?

Because right now, we were both lost.

And I didn't know how—or if—we'd find our way back.

.

Chapter Three

U nder the circumstances, I let Mitch sulk the rest of the afternoon, and I hadn't made the cancellation. Selfish, sure, but I wanted to celebrate our anniversary and figured it would be good for him. A distraction. Something to remind him we still had a life outside this curveball.

Besides, it couldn't be true. The child couldn't be his. The kid was younger than five, and we'd been together for five years. The math didn't work. And Mitch wasn't rich, not the kind of man you pinned with paternity to chase a cheque. Jasmine must've had some other reason for this bombshell. Until I knew what that was, I chose to believe in my man. At least for tonight.

I figured it would be good if Eric and Lily joined us and helped pull Mitch out of his spiral.

"Mitch," I said, sliding beside him on the couch.

His leg bounced. His thumb tapped the edge of his

phone screen, though he wasn't looking at it. Every few minutes, he'd rub his scalp like he was trying to dig through the problem with his fingertips.

"How about if our friends join us tonight?"

"I don't know." Barely a whisper. His voice was hoarse, like his thoughts had been shouting all day.

With a heavy and resigned sigh, I picked up the phone. Eric might have better luck getting through.

"Hello?" he answered over background noise of a wailing baby.

My stomach did a somersault. "Is that..."

"He arrived. Little baby boy."

My jaw dropped. Lily hadn't even been close to showing signs of an impending birth the last we heard.

"Already? Wow. Congratulations." I turned to Mitch, tugging at his sleeve as I lowered the phone. "They had their baby. A little boy."

"At least they knew about it," he muttered, eyes still locked on a spot on the floor.

My chest tightened and I recoiled.

"Mom and baby are healthy. Arrived just under an hour ago," Eric said, his voice flooded with joy.

"That's amazing. How's Lily?"

"Glowing and exhausted. Mitch okay?"

I tossed my gaze over him. He was not the same man I woke up to. "Not really. I was going to invite you out for dinner, but you clearly have more important plans."

"Raincheck for another night," Eric said. "Tell him congrats on the anniversary."

"Will do. Give Lily our love."

I hung up and stared at Mitch. He looked worn-out, like life had been chiseling away at him all afternoon.

"That's it. Get up." I smacked his leg. "We're going out."

His head jerked toward me, startled.

I jumped to my feet. "Damn it, Mitch, it's our anniversary, and we have dinner reservations. Tonight, you're going to put on your best suit, and we're going to do all the things we shouldn't because we deserve it. Do you hear me?"

He blinked and slowly gave me the faintest nod. "Yes. You're right. Today is a special day."

"Damn right. We deal with Jasmine tomorrow. Tonight, you're mine."

Thirty minutes later, we were ready. Mitch cleaned up well, always had. His navy suit hugged his frame just right, the bowtie crisp if not a little crooked. However, he still had that stormy look in his eyes, but at least he'd brushed his hair.

I threw on a jean jacket over my maxi dress and pinned my blonde waves up. Something a little different. A little bold.

Mitch turned toward me, his jaw slackening just

slightly. "You are gorgeous. But you're missing something."

I gave myself a once over. "Nope, I have everything."

He reached into his pocket and pulled out a long, black box.

My breath caught as I opened it.

Inside, nestled in velvet, was the tree of life pendant I'd pointed out months ago in a dusty corner of a local artisan's shop. Made of twisted metal threads, it was intricate and raw, each branch unique.

"Our birthstones," he said, pointing to the garnet and emerald worked into the roots.

My throat tightened. It was the perfect gift and in less than a year, we could add another stone—our child's—to the branches. "Help me put it on?"

He fastened it gently, his fingers lingering at the nape of my neck.

I turned and kissed him, slow and deep. "Thank you."

"Anything for you."

After the afternoon he'd had, I couldn't give him the old pencil case with the positive pregnancy test inside, but I had to give him something.

"Your gift," I purred, tracing his lapel, "will come later. A private show. You call the shots."

He raised a brow. A familiar smile tugged at the

corner of his mouth. "Anything?"

"Anything."

The light in his eyes flickered back to life.

He smacked my ass playfully. "Wear the red underwear."

I grinned, flipped up my dress, and flashed the lacy thong. "Already on it."

"It's going to be a quick dinner."

"Nope." I giggled, happy to have my man back. At least for the moment. "Delayed gratification."

He growled low in his throat, then traced a finger over my dress, circling my nipple through the fabric. I inhaled sharply.

"Not now, cowboy," I said, stepping away. "Let's eat first. I'm hungry."

The thirty-minute walk helped cool us both off— barely. The breeze smelled of sea salt and grilled fish, and the night air was warm against our skin. He held my hand tight, and I stole glances at him when he wasn't looking. There were still lines on his face, but at least his gaze had stopped drifting toward the horizon like he was waiting for an answer to walk up and explain itself.

We arrived just a few minutes late, but thankfully, the hostess hadn't given away our booth.

"What are we celebrating tonight?" she asked, walking us to our beautiful seaside table.

"Our anniversary," Mitch said, kissing the back of

my hand. "Five years today."

"Five years ago, I finally said yes to him, to be his girl," I added.

She smiled and handed us menus and then filled our water glasses. "Aww, that's sweet. Congrats. What can I get you from the bar?"

Shit. I panicked. I couldn't drink.

"Umm… a daiquiri?"

Mitch looked up from the menu; brow creased. "Really? Not a beer?"

"Something different. It's a big day."

Nodding, he turned to the hostess. "I'll have a draft."

When she took off, I excused myself under the guise of needing the bathroom.

On the way to the restroom, I flagged the hostess and whispered, "In my excitement, I forgot to add, I'm on new medication and can't have alcohol. Can you make mine virgin, please?"

Her expression didn't flinch. "Of course."

Back at the booth, I stroked Mitch's hand. The scent of garlic and citrus drifted from the kitchen. Soft lights hung above, swaying gently with the breeze. A candle flickered between us. The ocean rolled and splashed the waves against the embankment.

The band started playing, mellow at first. A low bass throbbed like a heartbeat.

I leaned into him. "I love you, Mitch."

He kissed the top of my head. "I love you too."

I slid my hand onto his thigh. Slow. Careful. He stiffened, then relaxed into it. His breath hitched when I grazed the hard ridge beneath his pants.

"Do you think this is the right place?" his whispered voice tickled my ears.

"Why not? Works in the movies."

He looked around, eyes calculating. The booth shielded us, and the music masked sound. I draped my leg over his. The heat between us sparked like live wires.

He slid his hand under the tablecloth, fingers finding their way beneath the lace. A shiver ran up my spine. I buried my face in his neck, biting back a moan as he circled that perfect spot.

"Oh, Mitch," I breathed.

My body tensed, pulsed, released. I grabbed his thigh to anchor myself, trembling with quiet ecstasy.

I kissed his jaw. "Your turn."

"Um," he pulled back. "Not here. I'm not leaving with soaked pants."

"Do you even know me at all?" I cocked a brow.

I craned my neck just enough to check our surroundings, then ducked under the tablecloth. His hand slid into my hair as I unzipped his pants.

He was already hard.

I wrapped my lips around him, slow and deep. My

rhythm was steady, practiced. Intimate.

He groaned, low and rough. His thigh muscles twitched under my hands. I pushed him higher, until he clutched the seat and hissed my name.

I emerged with cheeks heated from the flush of excitement.

"All clear?" I teased.

He adjusted himself and exhaled a laugh. "You're something else."

"Happy anniversary, honey."

I kissed him, savouring his exquisite taste and the thrill of our recklessness.

I felt reborn as I opened my clutch and popped a mint. My lips tingled, my cheeks were tinged with heat and no doubt, there was a sparkle in my eye.

Our food arrived, steam curling from roasted chicken and buttery vegetables.

"You are truly amazing," Mitch said, his voice husky. He kissed my hand again, lingering this time.

"I could say the same about you," I whispered, brushing my fingers down his cheek. I kissed him, soft and slow, searching for something in the warmth of his mouth.

He pulled back, tipping his head as he looked at me. "What's gotten into you tonight?"

"You don't like it?"

"I do. It's just… unusual."

"It's been an interesting day. Babies born, life changing. The air feels filled with something, doesn't it?"

He froze. A flicker of tension returned to his shoulders.

"Ugh. Babies. Don't even go there."

My pulse stuttered.

He shook his head. "I'm glad Lily had hers. But I'm not ready. Not interested. Never wanted kids."

I blinked. The words landed like cold water.

Never?

Five years. And I'd never known that.

Mitch reached for my hand again, but something cracked in my chest. Small. Subtle. The kind of crack that only gets wider with time.

Chapter Four

The mood around dinner took a sharp turn, like someone had pulled the rug out from under a good joke. I tried to tease Mitch into dancing with me—twirling a little in my dress, holding out my hands with a grin—but he barely cracked a smile. His eyes were far away, and his body moved like it weighed more than it should. Even his footsteps on the walk home had a heaviness to them that matched the cloudy evening with nary a visible star.

We passed a quiet little kids' park on the corner, the kind with peeling paint and creaky swings.

I tugged at his hand, coaxing him off the path. "C'mon. Let's go for a swing ride."

He gave me a look that was half confusion, half amusement. "We're too old. And it's dark."

"Perfect," I countered, tugging him towards the saucer swing. "You're only as old as you feel, and I feel young and vital." And pregnant, but that secret still sat between us, tucked away for another day. "Now, hop on."

He gave a resigned chuckle, letting me guide him onto the oversized swing. It creaked slightly under our weight, designed for four kids, so two adults with impure thoughts shouldn't be a problem. I crouched to give him a flash of my lace thong, the fabric catching the low light from the streetlamp.

His brows drew together, torn between arousal and concern. "Seriously, Cedar, what's gotten into you tonight?"

"I need you," I whispered, crawling onto the swing, my body pressing into his. The chains clinked softly as we rocked. "I need that connection."

His hand slid to my hip as I straddled him. "Let's go home. I'll give you whatever you want."

I kissed him, deep and messy, the kind of kiss that said I wasn't waiting for later. My breasts pressed against his chest, his body stiffening beneath me—not from reluctance, but need. My hand slipped down his front, found the button or his dress pants, and popped it open with practiced ease.

Mitch exhaled through his nose, his fingers rising to cup my breasts, then trailing down to my hem. He tested me with a slow stroke, and I arched against his touch.

"I'm all yours," I murmured, hot against his ear.

"Climb aboard the SS Macomber."

I giggled, breathless. "Aye aye, captain."

The first thrust made the swing jolt, setting us in motion. With every push of his hips, the saucer swung higher, the chains creaking in rhythm with our bodies. The night air licked at my skin, mixing the cool breeze with the heat blooming between us. My fingers tangled in his hair as I rode him, the weight of our bodies drawing us closer, tighter.

I saw stars, or maybe it was the motion, the height, the thrill of being tangled up with him like this, out in the open. I came hard and fast, gasping his name as my arms locked around his neck.

"So close," he panted, lost in my body.

I shifted, teasing out every inch of him until he groaned and followed me over the edge. The swing rocked wildly beneath us, and I held on tight as he peppered my chest with kisses, his body still trembling.

"Can we go home now?" he whispered, voice low and hoarse.

I crushed my lips to his, threading my fingers into his thick, damp hair. "Take me to bed or lose me forever."

He pulled back with a lopsided grin. "Show me the way home."

It was a quote from our favourite film, and judging by the look in his eyes, we were about to sprint the rest of the way.

* * *

The alarm shrieked too soon. I rolled over, stretching an arm across Mitch's bare chest to silence it.

"Hey, baby," I murmured, giving his earlobe a slow, lazy lick. "Time to wake up."

He groaned, keeping his eyes closed. "Didn't we just go to sleep?"

"Only a few hours ago."

My body ached in the best way. I felt deliciously used, stretched, satisfied. We'd rung in our anniversary with so many rounds I'd lost count, and I had no regrets. I'd kept him distracted—and I'd do it again if I had to.

"Coffee?" I asked, crawling over him, deliberately dragging my naked body across his. I straddled him, already feeling him stir beneath me.

"Damn, Cedar. We shouldn't."

"But we could." I cupped my breasts, watching his gaze darken. "We've got time."

"You're going to be the death of me," he muttered, though his hands gripped my hips, and his desire was already evident. "Edge of the bed."

He flipped me over effortlessly, his body heavy and hot as he drove into me. We weren't slow. We were on a mission. His thrusts were deep and urgent, our breath coming in gasps as we chased another high.

He reached it first with a hoarse groan. I followed close behind, fingers clenched in the sheets.

"We've need to get to work," he said with a lazy grin, giving my ass a firm squeeze before disappearing into the shower.

I followed, grinning like a fool.

* * *

We weren't even ten feet into the airport before we saw Eric standing at the desk.

"What are you doing here? Shouldn't you take the day off? Or the week?" I asked.

He looked like he'd barely slept, but not for the same reasons we hadn't. "Lily says she's fine. It's just one flight to YVR. I'll be back before lunch."

"Kavanagh can cover for you," Mitch said, already reaching for the phone.

"Honestly, I'm fine. Willow said babies sleep a lot in the first twenty-four hours, so let's see."

Willow was the local midwife, someone I really needed to get in touch with.

Eric winked, but it was tired, lingering. His defences were slipping.

I glanced between him and Mitch. "Flying while tired is just as dangerous as flying while drunk and Lily needs you to come back home safe and sound."

Mitch's voice broke the sudden silence. "Hey, it's Mitch. You free to do a hop to YVR?" He scanned the day's manifest. "Four passengers. Family, maybe. Cedar can sort logistics. Perfect, thanks." He hung up with a grin. "Done. Easy."

Eric let out a sigh and slumped into my chair, grateful. His loyalty was admirable, but he didn't have to prove anything today.

"Thanks," he murmured, filing the binder away.

"How did last night go?" he asked. "Did you call that woman? Find out what she wanted?"

"Uh, no. We were busy," Mitch said, eyes darting everywhere. "It was our anniversary."

"Oh, yeah, right."

I took the clipboard from him and gestured for Eric to get up. I needed to start prepping for the day.

As Eric stood, he gave the desk a couple of pats. "Who is she, anyway?"

My fingers hovered above the phone. I'd done everything to keep Mitch's mind off that woman last night. Now Eric had dragged her name back into the room, and just like that, the tension returned.

Mitch pushed off the counter and walked toward the back room without a word.

Eric and I watched him go.

"Whoever she is, he clearly doesn't want to talk about it," Eric muttered, straightening the pens on the edge of the desk.

I didn't either. Not really. That woman spelled

uncertainty. Danger. If Mitch already had a child out there—and didn't want one to begin with—my news would shatter him. I'd seen the flicker of fear in his eyes yesterday.

I wasn't ready to lose him.

Not yet.

Chapter Five

Two days later, I was wrung out. Emotionally drained, physically spent. The kind of exhaustion that didn't sleep off with a nap or vanish with caffeine. Mitch was just as worn down, maybe more so. He'd retreated into himself, withdrawn except for when I pressed him with sex—our one remaining thread of closeness. Even then, when it ended, he vanished again, distant and unreachable.

That morning, I sat beside him on the couch, searching his face for a flicker of the man I knew. "Okay, I can't keep doing this, Mitch."

He didn't flinch.

"Mitch?"

A heavy sigh filled the space between us, and he turned to acknowledge he'd heard me. "I know what you're trying to do. And I appreciate it—I think." Closing his eyes, he rested his head on the back of the couch. "But,

Cedar, love, I need a break."

A pang hit me square in the chest. "From me?" My voice cracked despite my best effort. I held my breath as tears poised on the edges, ready to burst free.

Head snapping up, he pulled me in without hesitation, wrapping his arms tight around me. "Oh, heavens, no. Never from you. I love you."

Relief surged through me, and I clung to him like a child.

"Who is she? Who's Jasmine?"

His chest rose beneath me, slow and deliberate, before letting the breath go with a sigh that sounded like surrender. "She's nobody important."

"Maybe not now. But she was once." I leaned back to meet his eyes, to see the truth—or the lie—lurking there.

"She's not important. Wasn't then, and sure as hell isn't now." His jaw tightened. "She's just causing trouble."

My sweet guy pushed away from me then, breaking the moment. Just like that. Gone again.

I agreed she was causing trouble, but the bigger question was why? Why now? Was she a troublemaker. Maybe? I didn't know her. And I'd learned better than to trust one person's version of a story. My best friend Lily had a rough past too, and people had labelled her all kinds of things. But people changed. They grew. Didn't they?

"You're not going to tell me anything about her?" I pressed. "She obviously knows you and knew you well."

His head snapped toward me. "Are you trying to pick a fight?"

"No. I'm just asking." My voice stayed even. Barely.

His voice pitched and he crawled out from under me, standing in front of the tv. "Then drop it, okay?" His tone sharpened; voice edged with something that sounded like panic. "I said she was nothing. Leave it at that."

He grabbed his keys from the dish near the door.

"Where are you going?"

"Out."

I was afraid to ask and did so with a shaky breath. "When will you be back?"

"I don't know."

The door slammed behind him. The sound rattled the pictures on the wall—photos of us at the beach, laughing over beers, holding hands at sunset. Moments that felt a world away now.

If he was going to shut me out, then I needed to figure things out on my own. I wasn't the same free-spirited girl I'd once been. I was a woman with something to lose and someone to protect.

Rather than sneak into the airport system and pull

Jasmine's personal details—although it was tempting—I took a higher, if shakier, road.

I walked down to Amber's Ale, a beachside pub my friend Amber owned and ran like a boss. Her place always smelled like cedar planks, rich beer, and salt air. The inside had a retro beach vibe, all polished wood and old surf photos, and the jukebox was already crooning the Beach Boys.

Amber looked up from behind the bar. "S'up, girl?" She reached for a pint glass.

"Not tonight." I stopped her before she poured my usual. "I need a clear head."

Her eyes narrowed as she studied me. "Everything all right?"

"No. I mean, I don't know. Maybe." I curled forward, leaning on the bar and clasped my head between my hands.

She gave a low whistle. "You are confused as all get out."

I nodded. Amber had always been the straight-shooting type. No bullshit. No coddling.

"Geez, you look like you're ready to cry."

Another nod as I looked into Amber's golden eyes.

"Not in my bar." She handed me a tissue, leaned in and lowered her voice. "You cry, and Denny's going to start in about his sister, and Georgina'll turn it into a great big therapy session. Before we know it, we'll have a damn support group on our hands."

An involuntary smile teased my lips as I sniffed. "Fair."

"So what's got your knickers in a twist?"

"Mitch."

She groaned, failing to hide her thoughts. "Frick. What is with men lately? Seriously—is it the weather? The water?" She took a sip of her drink. "So, what'll I get you to drink?"

"Just a Coke, please."

Amber nodded and poured the soda, adding a cherry on top like I was twelve. "All right. Spill it. Your thoughts, not the drink."

"I think Mitch had an affair."

There. I said it. Like popping a blister—sharp, necessary, and too late to undo.

I rubbed my face with my left hand and then rested my head in it.

"No shit. When?" Her voice dropped low.

"Years ago. And I only found out when she got off the plane... with their son."

Amber's mouth opened wide, then slammed shut as her expression darkened. "The dirty bastard."

My fingers tightly gripped the cool glass. "I wanted to dig into her file. Her name, where she's staying. Everything."

Eyes wide, she shook her head. "Please tell me you didn't. You'd get canned for that."

"I didn't. But I wanted to. Badly."

I traced my finger around the rim of my glass, trying to keep my thoughts in order.

"Oh, wait a sec, is she that uptight one with the kid I see around town?"

"Probably. Poor kid."

Amber scoffed. "If you're going to cheat, at least let it be with someone who looks like a fantasy. She's a dog."

I barked a laugh, surprised by it, because she wasn't unattractive at all, quite the opposite. "*Allegedly* he had an affair. Allegedly."

"And what exactly did the loser have to say about it?"

Amber had zero tolerance for cheaters. Her father cheated on her mother, repeatedly. Then her last boyfriend really did a number when he messed around. She only found out about his affair when she came down with a mysterious STD and had to have the talk with the jerk. Now, if infidelity is even so much as hinted it, her instant revulsion for the cheater in question is epic.

"First off, he's not a loser. I love him with all my heart." Mitch was my guy. We had dreams. Not married ones though, but still the together forever kind that didn't require a piece of paper. A couple of weeks ago we've even discussed the possibility of getting a dog. Only couples who were serious about longevity in their relationships did that, right?

A heavy sigh with the chill of an oncoming winter breezed out of Amber. "What did Mitch say?"

I sighed. "That she's not important. That she never was."

Amber shook her head, the unpins curls bouncing around. "Classic. If he's innocent, he'd say something real. He'd explain. Instead, he clams up. That's guilt, babe."

"I don't want to believe it. I love him." My heart constricted at the thought. Mitch was my everything, and he'd told me I was his. How could this have happened?

"Just because you love him doesn't make him innocent."

I sipped my Coke, bobbing my straw. "He didn't deny the kid. But he didn't confirm it either."

She jabbed a finger at the air. "Because he's guilty. Why can't guys commit? All of them, losers. Class-A losers."

"Awe, Amber. Not all of them are."

"Yeah, well, between you, Mom and me, we're not batting a 400." Her baseball terms went right over my head. "The jerk's not talking about it, eh?"

"I think he's in shock."

She tipped her head back as she laughed. "Yeah,

shock that he got caught. Excuse me."

Amber stepped away to pour a drink for a guy at the other end of the bar.

He tipped his hat at me. "Can I buy you one?"

I didn't make eye contact but stared back at his reflection in the mirror behind the bar. "Not interested. I have a boyfriend."

"Your loss."

I turned back to Amber. "Gross."

She sidestepped over and gave the bar a swipe with her cloth. She hated water marks on the bar. "So. What now?"

"I don't know. I never thought I'd have to share. Not him."

Amber tilted her head. "Is that what's really bugging you?"

I didn't answer. If I did, I'd cry.

Growing up on the commune, I shared everything—clothes, food, space. Even my parents, who practised free love and shared each other like borrowed books. I had a biological dad, sure, but I also had at least a half dozen siblings. I never had anyone just for me.

Until Mitch.

Back then, I didn't even know you could *catch feelings*. Sex was just... a thing we did. But here? With Mitch, it *meant* something. That's the part I wasn't ready for and I believed Mitch would be different. Was different. That we'd have something whole. Something untouched by the ghosts of the past.

Until Jasmine stepped off that plane and popped my perfect little bubble.

Chapter Six

I left Amber's bar more wound up than when I arrived. Somehow, her support had energized my anxiety, not soothed it. By the time I got back to the apartment, my feet throbbed from the long, angry walk home. I waited for Mitch, but my exhaustion finally won, dragging me into uneasy sleep on the couch.

When I opened my eyes, the sun was already up. I was still on the couch—but someone had draped a blanket over me. My heart caught for a second. Maybe he *did* come home, maybe he did still care.

I padded down the hallway and saw Mitch's keys in the dish. The bedroom door was open a crack. Inside, he was face-down on the bed, hogging most of the mattress like he always did. For a moment, I just stood there, watching him breathe, trying to read something— *anything*—in the curve of his spine or the slackness in his jaw.

Walking closer, I hovered my hand above his shoulder and pulled back in surprise. He stank of booze. Sharp and sour.

I punched him lightly. "Get up."

He didn't budge.

"Get *up*," I snapped, this time shaking him with more force. "You need to go to work."

Groaning, he rolled over, eyes barely open. "I'm not going in."

"Yes, you are. You can work off your hangover there."

"I said I'm not going." He tugged the blanket over his head like a child.

"Did you drive home drunk?"

"No," he mumbled. "Eric got me."

I froze. Eric? I narrowed my eyes into slits, reminding myself to thank Eric later. And to maybe verify the story. Mitch knew better than to drive home drunk but lately, he'd been different. Who's to say he didn't do it once because it wasn't that far of a drive?

My stomach clenched, and a fist of doubt curled inside my chest.

"Fine," I said, trying to steady my voice. "I'm taking the car."

"Whatever," he muttered, already halfway back to unconscious.

* * *

Dressed and ready to greet more tourists, although my heart wasn't into it this morning, I walked over to the car which was parked off kilter at an angle in our parking spot. Eric would never have left the car like that. In that moment, a knife to the heart would've hurt less. Mitch had lied.

I pulled in front of the tiny, seaside airport and surveyed the parking lot. Eric's car was parked closer to the edge of the building. A swirling of emotions mixed all up in me. I didn't want to confront Eric, he'd been a great friend to me and the best of friends to Mitch, so naturally I'd assume the guys would stay loyal to each other. I highly doubted I was going to get much information from him. Ugh.

My hand smacked the steering wheel in frustration, sending a jolt of pain up my wrist. Good. At least that pain made sense.

Hopping out of the car, I slammed the door so hard I almost hoped it would shatter the glass – maybe that would be the release I desperately needed. But I didn't and seeing it all in one piece calmed me for a fraction of a heartbeat. No doubt replacing the window would be an added expense I didn't need right now.

But what did I need?

Answers. So many answers.

Inside the building, I stomped to my desk and jabbed the power button on my computer, willing it to start up faster than its ancient bones allowed.

"Morning." Eric's voice behind me, casual as always, and amazingly bright-eyed and bushy-tailed.

I didn't turn. "Morning."

"Rough night?"

"As if you didn't know," I muttered, eyes narrowed as the login screen appeared. Angrily, I punched those keys hard and clicked the mouse hard enough to hear it crack as I signed in.

A beat of silence.

"I really don't."

I turned slowly. He looked genuinely confused and I knew Eric well enough to know he couldn't fake that kind of sincerity.

"Mitch said you drove him home last night, so I'm sure you know all about it."

Eric blinked. "He said what?"

"You didn't?" The question cracked my voice right down the middle and hollowed my words.

He shook his head slowly. "I haven't seen Mitch in two days."

The air left my lungs like I'd been sucker-punched. I dropped my gaze to the keyboard and clutched it like it might anchor me. My eyes stung. No crying. Not here. Not at work.

I willed myself to focus on the screen and click on what I needed to keep me from falling apart—today's manifest. Scanning the details, I hit print and took a deep, painful breath, begging myself to stay together.

Eric backed away like the heat of my reaction scorched him. "I'll get the bird ready. Can you print the schedule?"

"On its way," I said automatically. My voice sounded distant even to me. "But you have two flights. One across the island. One to YVR." Airline code for Vancouver, BC.

Eric froze when Billy, one of our mechanics, limped in and broke the moment. "What's going out today?"

"I'll double check nothing's changed."

Today's listing of passengers was neatly on display. Everything checked out, and so far, no cancellations. The printer ran through its motions and the manifest sat on the top.

Eric's eyes enlarged and he sauntered back over to my desk.

"Where's Mitch?" He kept his voice low as to not upset the other mechanic, who was older and only worked part time. Very part time. As in whenever someone called in sick.

"He stayed home nursing a hangover of epic proportions."

I thrust the clipboard into his hand and focused on the small tasks. Routine. Predictable. Safe.

Printing the day's documents, my hands still shook from everything I was holding back.

Eric grabbed the pages from the printer, and walked back to my desk, leaning close as he lowered his voice. "You two have a fight?"

"We're... something." I didn't even know what that meant anymore.

A long inhale through his nose, after which he nodded. "You know he loves you, right?"

I didn't answer.

"He wouldn't hurt you on purpose."

"It's not the *purpose* that hurts," I whispered. "It's the lies. The secrets."

Eric rested a hand gently on my shoulder, and it nearly undid me. "Come over tonight. Meet the baby."

I rolled my bottom lip between my teeth and dared to look anywhere but at Eric. Too afraid he'd see the chaos inside. Instead, I forced a weak smile and clicked away on the keyboard. "Do we get to know his name?"

"Come find out," he said with a soft grin. "I'll check with Lily."

He left me with that—something warm in a day already gone cold.

The terminal emptied out again. The morning rush faded into silence. Just me and the hum of old systems and fluorescent lights. My fingers hovered above the keyboard.

Now was my chance.

I told myself it wasn't wrong—this was security information. I had access. I needed answers.

Jasmine Coolidge.

There she was.

I clicked.

The screen populated with her full name, age, country of origin.

Nothing illegal yet. I could justify this. I had before.

But my cursor hovered over her *son's* name. My throat tightened. My pulse thumped wildly in my ears.

I had no right. No reason. Not yet.

And still... I clicked.

Chapter Seven

Shit! I clicked. In that nanosecond, nausea built at a speed I didn't know was possible.

Even though the pop-up screen was only there for a fraction of a minute—just long enough to catch the birthdate and commit the six digits to memory—the damage had been done.

I gathered the new information at warp speed, but now I was going down for breaking the law. I just knew it.

But I couldn't unsee what I saw, and before rational thought blew in and wiped it clean, I scratched the numbers down on a nearby notepad, circling them all, especially the year.

Four. The kid was four. Not five like I'd always believed. Just shy of four years and four months old.

Which meant, doing the math... conception happened *just as* Mitch and I got together.

Anger flared my nostrils wide and my breath ragged.

All this time, I'd doubted and hoped against hope that she, Jasmine, had been wrong. Amber had warned me too, and my gut had whispered truths I didn't want to hear.

And now, it was shouting.

Bastard.

I picked up the phone, hands trembling. The line rang and rang and rang.

Just as I was about to hang up, Mitch answered. "Hey, honey."

"Don't give me that honey shit." My voice was low and sharp, clenched between my teeth. "We need to talk. Tonight. No more deflections."

He didn't answer. Not really. But the line wasn't silent either.

A soft *shh*.

Then… a squeaky, high voice in the background. Asking for juice.

My heart stopped. "Is she there?"

"I can explain—"

"You brought her into our apartment? Without telling me?" My voice hit a register I didn't recognize.

"Let me explain."

"I've been *waiting* for you to explain. And now you let her into our *home*? With her *child*?" My hand shook as I slammed the phone down into the cradle.

My stomach flipped, once, twice, and before it went another time, I ran to the bathroom and threw up.

It was too much. Too fast. Sweat slicked my skin and clung to my clothes, and I would've blamed the flu if I didn't know better.

But I knew better.

Mitch had created a child with *her* — and said *nothing*. Nothing. And now she was in *our apartment*. The home I helped build, the life I thought I had some control over.

God. What the hell was I supposed to do now?

I rinsed out my mouth and stared at my reflection. Eyes wide, hair frizzed, jaw clenched so tight it hurt. This wasn't who I was supposed to be.

But it was who I'd become.

I had a shift to finish, and I still had to face Eric without falling apart. He was my rock, and I'd never kept anything from him — until recently. First the pregnancy, now this whole destructive bomb with Mitch. I was on a terrible streak for secrets.

No metaphorical escape door existed. So I inhaled, exhaled and forced my pulse to slow.

Work. That was the only thing that would save me from unraveling.

I buried myself in make-work projects until my focus was too occupied to dwell. The clock ticked forward, and finally, Eric returned from his first flight, beaming.

He held up his phone. "Wanna see the baby?"

"Duh." I rubbed my hands together and tried my best to be excited.

The tiny photo made me soften just enough. Those sweet cheeks. A tuft of light-coloured hair. A miracle wrapped in a swaddle.

"Lily says you can come by after supper. Quick visit though."

Perfect. Short and sweet. Exactly what I needed — a reminder that good things still existed in the world.

"I'll be there. With presents," I said, wiggling my eyebrows like the world hadn't just collapsed under my feet.

"Oh, can you bring the router, too. Mine's acting up again."

"Can you ask Mitch? I'm not going home after work."

Eric paused. "At all?"

I hesitated, wondering how much I was saying without saying a thing. Instead, I shrugged.

"Not until after I see you guys." Maybe not then, either. Maybe not ever. At this moment in time, I didn't have the answer. I didn't have any answers.

He tipped his head, studying me like he could see all the cracks forming. "All right. Anything you want to talk about?"

I shook my head and focused back on the screen, trying to act busy as my heart screamed.

But I didn't miss it. The soft sound of Eric's phone sliding from his pocket. The call button being pressed.

As he stepped out onto the tarmac, I heard him.

Loud and clear.

"What the hell is going on between you and Cedar?"

Chapter Eight

*a*n hour after dinner, I tiptoed up Eric's stairs just as the sun dipped behind the ocean like it had something to hide. Someday, I'd live in a house like this. A dream. More like a *retirement fantasy* with what I made — but who knew? Maybe I'd win the lottery before someone on this street gave up their family legacy.

Bags shifting in my hands, I rapped lightly on the screen door. Inside, a baby wailed. Poor little guy.

Eric appeared and pushed the door open with a soft smile. "Hey. Just give her a quick minute. She's just finishing feeding him."

"Oh, I can wait out here. Let me know when she's done." I took a step back, half-turning toward my car. I could kill time doom-scrolling or checking in on a dozen apps I'd been avoiding.

Eric followed me out. "No Mitch?"

"You tell me. You spoke to him last." I shrugged,

feigning indifference. "I haven't been home. Yet." I added, as if that would help.

He closed the door behind him and leaned against the railing. "I try not to interfere, but when my two best friends are acting like complete strangers, I get a little worried. What's going on?"

"Nothing." My tone was flat. Final. Like a slammed door.

Eric raised an eyebrow. "Cedar."

"Look, I don't want to talk about it, okay?" My voice cracked slightly, and I turned away before he could see too much.

"You talk to Lily yet?"

"No." I looked him square in the eye. "But I talked to Amber."

Eric let out a low whistle. "And Mitch is still alive? That's progress. Either that, or you didn't truly tell her what's going on."

Amber's disdain for most men was legendary — partly earned, partly weaponized. No one dared date her in this town anymore; it wasn't worth the bruised ego.

Lily's voice floated down the hall and out onto the veranda. "We're done! Come on in."

"Come see." Eric held the door for me. I ducked under his arm, my arms full of gifts leading the way inside.

Lily was in the living room, glowing like someone

had lit her from the inside.

I had to blink twice. "Damn. You look *amazing*."

She blushed, smoothing her shirt. "I still feel huge."

"Stop. You're gorgeous. Motherhood suits you."

And it wasn't just a compliment — she radiated warmth. If I still read auras, I'd say hers was the softest pink. I used to do that, read energy. Until Mitch started mocking it. Called it *witchy nonsense*. So I stopped although I hadn't forgotten.

But Lily? She glowed.

"You want to meet him?" she asked, gaze shifting down to her son.

"Obviously. But first—" I handed her the bags. "These are for you."

Her eyes widened as Eric took the baby from her arms. "You went way overboard."

"The store had the cutest stuff; I couldn't help it." A little flicker of joy sparked inside me — buying baby things made everything real. Eight months from now, I'd be doing this for *my* baby.

One by one, they pulled out the gifts: buttery-soft sleepers, a milestone frame, warm blankets, a pack of washcloths that felt like clouds.

"The lady at *Belles et Garçons* said you can never have too many," I said, watching Lily's eyes shine.

"Thank you," she murmured, setting the tiny

clothes aside to give me a hug. "He's going to be the best-dressed baby on the island. Ready to hold him?"

"Absolutely. Just let me wash up." The saleslady's voice echoed in my head — *always wash before holding a newborn.* She had the authority of a midwife and the attitude of a sergeant.

I returned a moment later, hands freshly scrubbed, arms out.

Eric transferred the tiny bundle into them gently. "Meet Henry Baker."

"Your quasi-nephew," Lily added.

"Henry. That's a great name," I whispered, my heart swelling. He stared at me with sleepy eyes, his blond fuzz catching the last light of the day. His nose was button-perfect, his pout delicate and soft. "He's breathtaking."

Right then, I knew I couldn't wait to meet my own child. Would they look like me? Or would they have Mitch's dark curls and too-charming dimples?

Henry stretched with a soft grunt, and something in my chest cracked wide open.

"Oh my god," I whispered. "I'm in love."

Lily looked up at Eric, who had a hand resting lightly on her shoulder. "Before he was born, I thought I knew love. But now that he's here?" She paused, smiling through tears. "I'd die for him. No hesitation. He's everything."

Her voice was steady, but her eyes shimmered. And it hit me then — she'd *earned* this peace. She'd clawed her way through the messy parts of her past and somehow found grace on the other side.

"I can't wait to have one of my own," I murmured, brushing my fingertip across Henry's cheek. "Tell me everything. Was the birth brutal? How was Willow?"

Eric snorted. "Willow almost missed the whole thing."

"I should've called earlier," Lily said, laughing. "But everything was steady — until it wasn't. And then, suddenly... he was coming."

"On the *beach*," Eric added with a shake of his head.

My eyes widened. "The *beach*?"

"Not ideal," Lily admitted, "but you know... it was beautiful in its own way."

"I'll never look at an ocean sunset the same." Eric rose. "Can I get you a drink?"

"Nah, I won't stay long. Just wanted a baby fix."

As I cuddled Henry closer, I caught myself cooing in baby talk and instantly cringed.

Lily laughed. "Everyone does that. Don't fight it."

I leaned in, breathed in that newborn scent — a mix of sunshine, milk, and magic. Completely intoxicating. But I didn't want to overstay.

With a sigh, I rose and pressed a kiss to Henry's

soft head and handed him gently back to Lily.

"You're leaving already?" she asked.

"Yeah. Need to check on Mitch." I winced; the words sour in my mouth. "He was nursing a hangover when I left this morning."

My eyes flicked to Eric. I hadn't asked where Mitch had been last night. But I'd been *thinking* it — all day. Had he been with her? With Jasmine? The thought made my stomach sour.

I kissed Lily's cheek and hugged Eric. "Let me know when I can come back. I need more of this."

"Anytime," Lily said, already cradling Henry like a pro.

She started to rise, but Eric gently eased her back down and kissed the top of her head. It was the kind of kiss that didn't ask for anything. Just gave.

It punched me in the heart.

That used to be me and Mitch — before the lies. Before the secrecy. Before Jasmine and Jackson.

We'd been messy, sure. But we'd been *real*.

Now? I didn't know what we were anymore.

Chapter Nine

y hands were trembling as I dug blindly through my purse for my keys. I hadn't been home since that morning, and dread twisted like barbed wire in my gut. Every step toward the door felt heavier. I wasn't sure what I'd find on the other side—or if I was strong enough to face it.

The key scraped against the lock. I shoved the door open, and a wall of floral scent smacked me in the face.

Dozens of bouquets filled the kitchen table, spilled across the counters, and crept into the living room like guilt in petal form.

Mitch was on me in seconds.

"Oh, thank God you're okay." His arms wrapped around me, warm and firm and *so familiar*. His woodsy cologne stirred something traitorous in my chest.

As much as I wanted to melt into him, I pushed

him away. Hard. "Of course I'm okay."

His relief didn't match my mood. He looked like a man who'd narrowly survived a crash. Me? I was still in freefall.

The flowers screamed louder than he did. Mitch only ever bought flowers when he'd fucked up. And this? This was a warehouse-level apology.

"I called you, over and over—texted, left messages—" He stayed back now, four feet of space between us. A safe distance. Smart.

I pulled out my phone. Messages, voicemails. He wasn't lying.

"I have some explaining to do," he said, standing stiff, like he already knew I might never forgive him.

"You *do*." The door slammed behind me, and a picture frame rattled against the wall, off-kilter like my world. I crossed my arms and held tight. "How *could* you?"

"I can explain. And you have every right to be furious."

I was already there. My blood was lava. My pulse pounded in my temples.

"Let's talk in the living room," he said gently.

The kitchen walls were too thin. We'd learned that the day our neighbor moaned her boyfriend's name loud enough for Mitch to greet him accordingly in the hallway.

I walked into the living room and counted three

more arrangements. A giant one on the coffee table and two on the side tables. The couch cushions had been fluffed. The room *smelled* like apology and bleach.

"What's up with Jasmine?" I asked, the name sharp and metallic on my tongue, wondering which of the cushions she had sat upon.

"Jasmine is... an old friend."

"How old?"

"From high school."

My arms crossed over my chest. "You didn't go to high school in Seattle."

"She lived here. On the island."

I narrowed my eyes. "She doesn't look like she's ever set foot in a town like this."

"It's true." He gestured toward the couch. "Please, just sit."

"I'll stand, thank you." Not until I disinfected everything.

Besides, I hadn't taken off my purse or shoes. I didn't know if I'd be staying more than five minutes.

"She's from Campbell River," he said, voice low.

"And?"

"You asked."

"I asked *why she's here*. Now. And in our apartment."

My head throbbed like a drumbeat under a thunderstorm. I pinched the bridge of my nose.

"Headache?" Mitch asked.

"Yes."

He disappeared into the kitchen and returned with a can of coffee grounds. "Smell this."

I stared. This man—the one who just detonated my life—still remembered my triggers. Still wanted to help.

I inhaled. The coffee scent cut through the florals, but my chest still ached. "So... is the child yours?"

"Yes." No hesitation. He didn't even blink. "Jackson is my son."

The world tilted. A heavy blanket of damp coldness draped over me. A scream built in my lungs and clawed at my throat. I pressed my lips shut so hard it hurt.

"When?" I finally barked out.

"After you and I started dating," he said quietly. "Before we... committed."

The words detonated.

I grabbed a pillow and hurled it across the room. Missed. Grabbed another. Threw it harder.

"You *cheated*! You don't get to weasel out of that with timelines!" Rage boiled my blood. "You are a jerk of the highest order. How could you?" I stormed back to where I came in.

Mitch ran to the door ahead of me and blocked me from leaving.

"Get out of my way!"

"NO!" In my years with Mitch, there were only a handful of times he ever raised his voice. I'd add this time to that list.

Mitch stepped between me and the door. His jaw was set, eyes pleading. "Please. Let me explain everything. Then you can go. Hell, I'll help you pack if you want."

I narrowed my eyes. "You're serious?"

"As a heart attack."

"Fine." I stomped my foot, downstairs neighbours be damned.

I stayed standing. He stayed leaning against the door like a man bracing for impact.

"Yes, it happened. That night with Jasmine. But I didn't go looking for it. I was in Campbell River helping a buddy with a plane restoration project. Jasmine was there. We used to be close. She invited me out. It was... familiar. Easy."

My hands balled into fists. "And I wasn't?"

"That's not what I mean." He pushed off the door, but didn't step closer. "You and I — Cedar, *you* scared the hell out of me."

I blinked. "Excuse me?"

"You were different. You made me *feel* something, and I didn't know what to do with that. Every time I leaned in, you pulled back. You barely looked at me the weekend we went to Victoria."

"I was trying to figure out if I could trust you!" I shouted.

"I didn't know that. All I saw was a girl who wouldn't let me in — not really. And yeah, I got scared. I thought I was imagining it. I thought maybe you weren't into me the same way. Jasmine was just... noise. But you? You were the song stuck in my head."

I squeezed my eyes shut. His words shouldn't matter. Not after what he'd done.

"I came home early," he added softly. "From Campbell River. Left the next morning. All I wanted was to be back near you. And that night when you made that dinner, when you said you were ready — Cedar, I was ready too. I knew I wanted you."

I opened my eyes. He was trembling.

"And you didn't think to *mention* that you'd just slept with someone else?"

"I didn't think it mattered." He flinched as he said it. "Until that dinner, you and I weren't official yet. I thought—I hoped—what we had could start clean."

"You thought wrong." My voice cracked. "You *let me* walk into something real, thinking it was just the two of us."

"I swear to God, I didn't know about Jackson until Jasmine showed up last week." His voice broke, and for the first time, I saw the fear behind his eyes. "She found me because of that airport article. She wants to move permanently to Seattle and needs my signature to legally relocate Jackson out of the country. That's why she came. After giving birth, she'd listed me as the father on the documents, so I have to do it."

"Why did you bring her here?"

"I panicked. I didn't know how to explain any of this without making it worse."

"Oh, *you did* make it worse," I snapped. "You brought her into *our home*. That's beyond disrespect."

"I know."

"I didn't even *want* a relationship," I said, my voice rising. "Not until you. And you made me *want* things. A future. Stability. Roots."

"I wanted that too."

"Then you shouldn't have touched her."

"I thought about what you told me — about how you didn't know how to feel things back then. I was scared too. I didn't know how to *trust* what we had. I messed up, Cedar. But I never stopped wanting you."

Silence hung between us. Heavy. Devastating.

Shoulders sagging, Mitch finally said, "I didn't want kids. I never saw that kind of life for me. But now there's a boy and, like it or not, he's mine. I don't know what the hell I'm doing."

"Well, you can figure that out on your own."

I turned for the bedroom, grabbed my weekend bag, and stuffed it haphazardly. My hands were shaking again. From rage. From heartbreak.

"Where are you going?" His voice sounded poised on the edge of control.

"I don't know yet. And you don't get to ask."

He followed me to the door, but didn't try to stop me.

"Cedar — I love you."

I looked at him. Broken, scared, stupid Mitch. And I *had* loved him too.

But love wasn't always enough.

I opened the door and walked away.

Chapter Ten

"'ll break his bloody neck." Amber paced in her living room. Her apartment was above the pub, so when I arrived at the bar with red eyes and tear-stained cheeks, she escorted me up, leaving her assistant in charge. "I swear to God if he shows his face around here, I'll kick his ass."

"Don't." My heart was already shredded — I didn't need Amber setting fire to the scraps.

I loved Mitch. That was the worst part. Because even though I wanted him to hurt, it had to come from me. And it had to mean something. "Don't bother."

"What did I tell you? All men are filthy pigs."

I burst into tears. Maybe some guys were, but Mitch wasn't. He'd been nothing less than perfect for me. He treated me right, he took care of me, he loved me with abandon. However, he had made a mistake and by not being honest about it, it had cost him. Because he lied about it. Because he had an affair when we were first getting together. It cost us. The worst part was hearing him breathe out how he never wanted children. What was I going to do now?

Amber fell onto the couch beside me. "Men are jerks. Every. Single. Guy."

"Not all, I promise."

"Yep. Think Lily caught the last good guy."

"They really are cute together." Even though my last visit with them was brief, it was easy to tell how well they fit together. Cliché, but true, they were like pieces of a puzzle. And now they had a baby, although the kid was Lily's, and not biologically Eric's. "Have you met the little one yet?"

"Nah. We're not that close. Lily and I go way back, but I think she'd rather forget those years."

"You knew Lily back then?"

I hadn't been privy to much about her teenage years, but Lily had mentioned how much of a spoiled brat she was, and how reckless she'd been with her youth. It was hard picturing her that way when all I saw was the sweetness in her and the way she made Eric happy.

"We never ran in the same circles, but our paths crossed a few times. She was a rebel with guys flocking to her ready to assist in her wild ways, whereas I needed to prove I could swim in a sea of blood thirsty sharks." There was bitterness on the tip of her tongue, but it was brief. "But whatever. I don't hold a grudge against her, and I think she's made amends to her past. At least she owned up to it."

Amber held grudges, but they were against her family, namely the brother she refused to talk about and the parents who no longer talked with her – something I completely understood after being outcasted from the commune.

"Yeah, Eric said she's more than made amends and the town seems to have let it go. Finally. Did Eric know her before, in those teenage days?"

Amber nodded. "They lived next door, but he was gawky and awkward, and they too ran in completely different circles. Took a while to grow into himself."

"Sheesh. I always feel so left out. You all would've been fun to be around."

"Oh, it was fun for sure. But we all did something wild in our pasts. I'm sure you weren't all squeaky clean on the commune."

"I was." Sad but true.

Living in the commune was even tighter than living in a small town. I couldn't sneeze without someone knowing. And if I was in a bad mood, there were too many people suddenly available to help me cheer up, usually with something *natural* but I never went for it, choosing instead to pour my thoughts into poetry and hiding my journal so the words would never be read aloud in nightly group.

When I moved away at seventeen—and shunned, never able to return—I learned my lifestyle wasn't common and most of my friends had a wildly different upbringing. It was a huge shock to the system when I found Cheshire Bay, a town full of people and private buildings and items that belonged to individuals and not the group as a whole, but I embraced the lifestyle. It was still laid back, but I learned new skills thanks to the patient people of the garden center and thankfully I was a quick study when it came to computers.

"You never smoked weed?" She tipped her head to the side and studied me while I shook out a no. "Want to now?" Amber rose and went to her kitchen, returning a heartbeat later with her smoke. Lighter in hand, she went to flick it on. "This'll be fun."

I put my hand out to stop her. "I can't."

"Oh, don't worry. It's very relaxing."

Relaxing was an understatement. I remember how the elders would zone out. "Yeah, it's not that."

The lighter flared beneath the cigarette but never ignited. "What's the problem? You'll be safe – I won't let you jump out a window or anything."

Even I knew weed didn't cause that kind of a reaction.

"Amber…" I held my breath because Mitch was supposed to be the one who found out first.

I almost didn't say it. Speaking it out loud would make it real. Would make *everything* real — the betrayal, the broken dreams, the whole tangled mess of love and lies. But Amber was staring at me, waiting, no judgment in her eyes. Just that fierce loyalty that always made me feel safe.

"I'm pregnant."

Her whole face lit up and her eyes grew wide as they scanned down my body. "You're pregnant?"

I nodded, a slight smile building. It felt good to finally share the news with someone. "*Just* pregnant. I found out on Tuesday."

"Yay!" Amber jumped up and down, and then her smile slid off as she fell back beside me. "Oh, shit. Mitch and Jasmine and Jackson."

"Yeah."

"That does put a damper on things, doesn't it? He doesn't know yet either, am I right?"

"I was going to tell him that night. It was our five-year anniversary, but she decided to show up and kibosh my plans." I sighed and my head hit the back of the couch. "That's not fair. She'd didn't plan to ruin my happiness. Hell, she probably didn't even know I existed."

"Wow." Amber tossed the smoke and lighter onto the coffee table. "You're a nicer person than I am."

"No."

"Yeah. I'd torch the bitch, not literally of course,

but I'd roast her." She looked at me, really looked, and her face softened. "But I know that's not what you need right now. Sorry."

"She doesn't know anything about me. Mitch did."

"Then he's the bastard. But I'm still giving her side-eye on principle. And I'll kick his ass nine ways to Sunday if I ever see him again."

I picked at a scab on my knee, picking the edges of it until it hurt and bled. "The only fault I have with Jasmine is her not telling Mitch sooner. That's what I don't understand."

"You said it was because she's moving to the US?"

"Yeah. I guess she needs his signature on the documentation stating Mitch gives approval for his kid to live there. It's all messed up and weird."

"Just curious, and don't answer if you don't want to, but…" Amber took a deep breath. "Would you have rather found out now that he fathered a child, found out years later, or would you rather you never knew?"

"Isn't there an option of *I wish he hadn't knocked her up*?"

"That's already happened."

I shrugged. The truth hurt.

"But since it did… which option is the best?"

"I don't know. It's already been four years, but…

Oh, I don't know." There was no easy answer. All of them were bad. "I hate that it happened. I hate that he lied to me or withheld the truth. I hate that he had her over to our home, without telling me or asking for permission." Tears burst free, and I crossed my arms over my chest to hold myself together. "This was supposed to be an amazing time for Mitch and me. We were supposed to be daydreaming about baby names and buying tiny shoes and arguing over stroller colors. Instead, we're falling apart."

"When *are* you going to tell Mitch?"

I looked over at my best friend, raising my shoulders in the process. "I don't know."

"You have to tell him. Otherwise, you'll be just like Jasmine, and if you continue to live in Cheshire Bay, Mitch will find out."

"I thought you hated Mitch."

A smile sprang to the corner of her mouth. "Oh, I do, and I'll never forgive him for upsetting you like he has. But if you don't tell him, then you're a Jasmine too."

Man, I hated when she pointed out the obvious. "I promise I'll tell him before the baby is born."

She cocked her eyebrow and gave me her best don't mess with me look. It was terrifying.

"Fine. Sometime within the next couple of weeks. Maybe when I go back and pack my things."

"You're going to move out?"

"Do I have a choice? I can't be with a guy who doesn't want kids." I sat on the edge of the couch.

There was so much to think through. When I found out I was pregnant, I was thrilled to picture our future together and now I needed to side-step the dream and plan the future of bringing up the baby alone. It was absolutely mind-boggling. Thank goodness I had eight months to prepare.

Chapter Eleven

There was a bouquet on the corner of my desk when I came into work, a riot of lilies, carnations, daisies, and red roses—beautiful and bold and completely unwelcome. It had been three days since I walked out. Three days of silencing my phone, ignoring the pings, refusing to read the messages. Three days of pretending to not see him moving around on the tarmac, or waltzing into the terminal, always feigning I needed to be somewhere else rather than within any distance of him. But there's only so many places to hide in the tiny airport. It hurt too much to see him, like a phantom limb I hadn't realized I'd lost until it ached.

The daisies grinned at me as I sat down and logged in, their white faces bobbing in the breeze from the nearby fan. I reached out and turned the vase around—let them smile at the passengers instead.

Today was busy. Four inter-island flights, two

inbound from the mainland, and one outbound to Seattle. My eyes scanned the manifest and I exhaled—Jasmine's name was listed on the outbound flight. At least one nightmare was boarding a plane today.

"Hey."

I jumped.

Mitch stood beside my desk, close enough to catch the faint scent of sawdust and detergent clinging to his clothes. His baggy overalls made him look boyish, but the shadows under his eyes told another story. He looked like hell.

"Good grief." My voice wavered even as I tried to sound annoyed.

"Sorry. I didn't mean to scare you." There was sympathy in his tone.

"No, it's fine." I dropped my gaze to the computer screen, pretending to be absorbed. As if it could tell me how to forget him. As if that were even possible.

"The flowers are for you, in case you couldn't tell by the card." He leaned on the ledge above my workspace, his knuckles white against the wood.

I had missed seeing the card buried in the depths of the floral arrangement, but I wasn't going digging for it now.

"Thanks." I kept my tone flat and professional, as if I were dealing with someone other than the man I had wanted to spend the rest of my life with.

He reached out, hesitated, and withdrew his hand like I was a flame. "I'm really sorry. You were right. I should've told you."

I shot out of my seat, my muscles tensing from my neck all the way to my toes. "What would you have said, Mitch? *'Hey Cedar, while I waited for you to decide if you wanted to be with me, I went and slept with someone else... and oh, by the way, I got her pregnant*'?" My voice cracked at the end, breaking under the weight of my betrayal.

The terminal was quiet, save for the overhead fan. Only Eric decked out in full uniform, who strode in as I reveled all, broke the silence.

"Morning," he said casually, ignoring—or pretending to ignore—the emotional standoff playing out in front of him.

I slid back into my chair, trying to calm my trembling fingers as they danced over the keyboard. When the schedule came up, I ripped the printouts from the tray and slapped them onto the clipboard.

"Busy day," I muttered.

I shoved the board into Eric's hands, trying to avoid Mitch's looming presence. "YVR, then to YQQ and back."

Eric squinted at the list. "SEA?" SEA was the airport code for Seattle, the plane Jasmine and her son were on.

"Is that you or Tahigan flying?" I asked, referring to another regional pilot.

"I thought I was. Let me double check." He wandered away, phone already at his ear.

I just wanted the other woman gone. Let her take her secrets and baggage and disappear into the clouds. Maybe take Mitch with her.

Or maybe not.

"Jasmine's leaving today," Mitch said quietly. Was that sadness in his tone, like a version of grief? That woman cost him so much by showing up to Cheshire Bay unannounced and carrying more baggage than allowed.

I didn't answer.

"She's... she's really a nice lady."

That did it. I grabbed a pencil, snapped it in half with a sharp *crack*, and flung the pieces into the trash. "As you've mentioned."

He winced. "You'd like her if you gave her half a chance."

"You're kidding, right?" I stood so quickly the chair squeaked against the floor. "You think I'd *like* the woman who wrecked us?"

His face crumpled, like he hadn't expected my anger to still be this sharp. "What do you mean, wrecked us?"

"I'm moving out, Mitch. We're over." My voice faltered. "I thought that was clear."

"No." He straightened, suddenly alert. His posture shifted from defeated to determined. "We're not breaking up. You needed time, and I gave you, and I'm still giving you, space to think. But this? You can't just throw us away."

"I'm not throwing anything away." I pressed both hands flat on the counter, grounding myself. "*You* did that. Before we even really got started." My voice dropped, heavy and slow. "You lied. You cheated. You betrayed me."

Each word landed between us like a blow.

"That was years ago." He pinched the bridge of his nose, looking like a man caught in a vice.

"And it still happened. And whether you like it or not, now you have her in your life. And you have a child. With her." My throat burned as I pushed the words out.

"I didn't ask for her to get pregnant."

"No," I whispered, "but it happened. And now, for the rest of our lives, we'll *know*. Every time you look at a kid playing soccer or riding a bike, won't you wonder what Jackson is doing? If he's like you? If he's yours?" My bottom lip took the brunt of my frustration and my hands trembled.

A flicker crossed his face—grief, maybe? Or guilt?

"I hadn't really thought about it," he said, but the words rang hollow.

"Well, I *have*. I've thought about *all* of it. And now I'm stuck wondering what that means for *us*—if there even *is* an us anymore."

He exhaled loudly. "I never thought I'd be a dad. Even when we got serious... I just figured we were enough. You and me. We were happy. We had a good life."

"We *did*." My voice caught. "But I always thought there could be more. I wanted more."

Eric returned; his brows drawn low. "You two need to finish this later. We've got guests."

Mitch backed off. "Yeah. Sorry."

So much for keeping things professional. I swallowed down the ache in my throat. "Won't happen again."

I forced my budding anger into the pit of my stomach to let it rot and pulled from the depths of my soul a smile. There was no warmth in it, but I forced it to stick to my face anyways as I headed over to greet the couple with my clipboard in hand.

I had barely taken ten steps before Mitch caught my hand.

"Please," he said. "We *have* to talk. I'm not letting you go until we do."

"But I have to work." My head bobbed from looking at him, over to the incoming guests and back.

"Please. Let's talk. Tonight." His voice dropped,

low and vulnerable. "Cedar, I found the red box with my name on it. The one that said *happy anniversary*. I know."

Chapter Twelve

itch walked outside, turning back once. I still hadn't managed to pick my jaw up from the floor. Why did he open the red box? I had hidden his gift in my drawer… and in my haste to slam my clothes into the bag, it must've fallen out. Damn. And his name was on it, along with a tag that read *Happy Anniversary*, so why shouldn't he open it?

Double damn.

"Ah, Miss?" The older woman called out to me, and I startled, blinking as though I'd just come out of a haze.

"Yes, sorry."

"There's no mechanical issues, are there?"

I straightened up, trying to shove my scattered thoughts into some kind of order. "I can assure you the plane you'll be riding in is a fine piece of aeronautical engineering. Let's get you all set up and ready to go."

My hands moved on autopilot as I inputted their info into the computer, tagged their bags, and added them to the trolley.

"Your captain will be out in a few minutes and your flight will be taking off as scheduled. In the meantime, why don't you have a seat over there and help yourself to any drinks?"

They nodded and shuffled off with their personal items, and as soon as they were seated, I bee-lined to the water cooler. My hands trembled as I poured a small cup and tipped it back. Cold. Sharp. I chased it with two more, like I could drown the tension coiled tight beneath my ribs.

Between processing passengers, I paced between the desk and the tarmac door, wearing a path in the concrete that hadn't been there yesterday. I should've felt relief that Mitch knew. That the secret wasn't festering in my gut anymore. But instead, all the pressure that had been pent up inside me just... shifted. Moved into my shoulders, my neck, the pounding behind my eyes. I caught my reflection in the smudged glass panel— shoulders hunched, jaw clenched tight, lips pale from pressing them together too hard. I didn't look like myself.

But the worst part of my day hadn't even hit me between the eyes yet.

Eric was refueling his plane when *she* walked into the building.

At the end of her arm was her child—Mitch's son—dragging a suitcase almost bigger than he was.

"C'mon, Jackson," she said, sounding more tired than annoyed. Her voice was soft around the edges, like it had been eroded by a long day.

Jackson looked like he'd already clocked out. Sleepy eyes, one shoe half untied, his hair sticking up in the back.

"Hi," she said, placing her purse on the counter with a sigh. "We're heading to Seattle."

I gave her a neutral smile, all professionalism and no heart. There was no flicker of recognition in her eyes. Just another ticket agent doing my job. She didn't know.

There was no malice and no awareness. But my stomach still bottomed out.

"I'll just need your information and your bags." I stepped around the desk and crouched next to Jackson. "Can I take your bag, buddy? Do you have your Mr. Fluffy?"

Jasmine's brows lifted. "You remember that?"

Looking up, I gave her a small smile. "Of course. All our visitors are important to Cheshire Bay."

That was a lie. I didn't remember everyone. But I'd remembered *her*. Even back then, something about her had felt like a loose thread I should've paid more attention to.

"I could use someone like you on my team." She

winked, then paused, her eyes narrowing just slightly as she took in my face. "Wait… you look… You're Mitch's girlfriend, aren't you?"

The air around me thickened. My skin flushed hot and cold at once. My throat tightened, and I forced a swallow past the rising lump.

"I'm so pleased to finally meet you," she said brightly. "Mitch said you were visiting a friend, so I'm sorry we didn't get to meet and hang out."

She lit up like we were old friends who'd just missed the chance to braid each other's hair and swap stories over coffee. Meanwhile, I was still internally face-planting.

"Jackson, honey, why don't you go and have a seat on the couch?" she said, smoothing a hand over his head.

He nodded groggily and shuffled over, curling up like a kitten on the armrest.

"Is he okay?" I asked, my voice softer than I intended, flicking my gaze between mother and son.

"I gave him some Gravol," she whispered. "He doesn't travel well. This way, he'll sleep for the flight and hopefully not throw up all over the captain's shoes." She gave a tired laugh and rubbed her temples. "No idea where he gets that from. Mitch, maybe? Does he travel well?"

I wanted to laugh. Or cry. Or both.

Hell no, Mitch didn't travel well. But it wasn't my information to give away. Not anymore.

"That's okay, you don't have to answer." She gave me a knowing smile. "I'm sorry if my being here has caused any tension between you and Mitch. He speaks so highly of you—how much he's in love. It's wonderful seeing him so happy. He's a great guy, and I'm thrilled he's found his special someone."

I blinked at her. Did she not realize? Or did she just choose to handle the awkwardness with this much grace?

She reached out and squeezed my hand—my actual hand—and I just stood there, letting it happen, heart hammering behind my ribs.

"I promise, we're—Jackson and me—we're not going to be a pain in your side," she said. "I'm not after him for any child support. I've even offered to have legal papers drawn up once I'm back at the office so he can give up his rights if that's what he wants. I have a great job with fantastic benefits and I don't need anything from him. Just, unfortunately, these forms signed." She tapped her bag. "Like I've told Mitch—and I'll say the same to you—you can be as involved or uninvolved as you want, there are no hard feelings on my end. In hindsight, I should've left the paternity part blank. Would've saved a lot of unnecessary heartache, and I'm so sorry if my arrival put any kind of a wedge between you. Oh gosh,

I'm rambling now. Sorry."

I swallowed hard. My heart felt like it was trying to fold in on itself.

She took a breath and gave me a genuine smile, the kind that crinkles in the corner. "If you're ever in Seattle, you've got a guest suite waiting, so promise me you'll use it."

After blinking at the unbelievable, I shook my head and then switched it to a nod. "Thank you. That's... very kind."

I handed her the boarding passes with fingers that didn't feel like my own.

Just then, a group of new passengers filed into the building, and I couldn't have been more grateful for the excuse to disengage.

"Have a safe flight."

"Thank you," she said with a warm, genuine smile, then turned to gather Jackson from the couch.

Mitch was right. She seemed like a decent person. Much more welcoming than I'd been. I probably came off as some glacial, uptight girlfriend. But how *was* I supposed to react? Welcome her with a bouquet and matching mom-patches for the kid's jacket? That wasn't me. That wasn't real.

* * *

Before I left work, I couldn't shake the ache in my chest.

Guilt. Shame. Exhaustion. I was so tired of lying awake at night, staring holes in the ceiling, waiting for the sky to fall.

I picked up the phone and dialed my boss. He answered on the second ring.

"Hey, Mr. Tyler, it's Cedar Ratzloff from Cheshire Bay Airport."

"Good afternoon, Miss Ratzloff. What can I do for you?"

My hand gripped the cord so tightly it left a dent in my skin. "Well, sir, I wanted to let you know that there was a data breech in the system."

"A data breech? When? We'll need to get IT on this." He was twitchy, and his voice was jumping all over the place.

"You won't need to get IT on it." Sweat burst in my armpits and nausea settled over me. "It was me, sir. I logged on." I rattled off the time and date. My voice barely shook, but inside, I was unraveling. "IT would be able to confirm it. I accessed a passenger's personal information for non-emergency reasons."

I held my breath, expecting to be immediately fired, and deservedly so. Tomorrow I'd be out looking for a new job, any job, to make sure the bills were paid.

A sigh of relief crossed over the line. "That's all?"

"Yes, sir." I nodded my head, not that he could see it.

More silence. The kind that makes your skin crawl.

"Just the one time?"

My breath hitched, and there was a thickness in my throat as if I were being strangled. "My screen showed the information for less than five seconds." I gave the passenger's name as well.

"Five seconds, eh?"

"Yes. I'm so sorry." I twisted in my seat, curling deeper into myself.

"You sound pretty guilty, Miss Ratzloff."

I breathed through the nausea curdling in my gut. "Guilty doesn't even cover it."

Typing continually clicked on his end.

"You've been a solid employee," he finally said. "If this is a one-time lapse, and IT confirms what you said... I think the best option here, would be to place you on probation."

Probation. Not fired. I blinked hard.

"Thank you," I said. "That's more than fair."

He hung up, and I sat in stunned silence, the receiver still in my hand.

I wasn't fired. I still had a job. I'd told the truth, and somehow, the world hadn't collapsed around me.

He hung up, and I sat in stunned silence, the receiver still in my hand.

I wasn't fired. I still had a job. I'd told the truth,

and somehow, the world hadn't collapsed around me.

* * *

Mitch entered through the tarmac door, brushing dirt off his hands. "YQQ is off. She's gone now."

I nodded, heart skipping.

He stepped closer, waving a hand in front of my face like I was a mannequin.

"Hey."

"Oh. What? Hey."

"You okay?"

The question was simple, but the answer was tangled and heavy.

He looked at me like he already knew. Maybe he did.

"Are you finished work soon?"

"Umm, yeah." I clicked into my system and sent the final paperwork to the printer.

"Great. Can I pick you up from Amber's place in an hour?"

"You'll have to, I left you the car." My voice has zero inflection, but his had a quiet edge, firm and low. Not demanding—just *decided.*

"Gimme one hour."

And with that, he turned and disappeared through the hangar door.

I logged out, barely feeling my fingers, and grabbed my bag.

My stomach fluttered with a weird mix of dread and something dangerously close to hope. He wanted to talk. And despite everything, I wasn't ready to close the door yet.

Mitch was a hard man to let go of.

Harder still to stop loving.

Chapter Thirteen

ou're late," I said quietly.

Mitch stood just inside the door of Amber's Ale, his hands jammed in his pockets, his body stiff. His hair was brushed back like he'd tried—really tried—to look the part of a man who could fix things. He wore a clean button-down and slate-grey pants, but he looked out of place. Unsteady. Like someone bracing for a storm they knew they deserved.

"I know." His voice was rough, eyes scanning my face like he didn't quite believe I was real. "I almost didn't come."

"Then why did you?" My throat betrayed me—scratchy, fragile. Just like the rest of me.

He opened his mouth, then shut it. His jaw clenched, his fingers twitching by his sides. "Because I owe you more than an apology. I owe you the truth. And maybe a few broken ribs, if that's still an option."

I didn't smile. Not yet.

Amber came around the bar like a tornado in flats. "Oh no. Out. Not in my place, not like this."

I slipped off the stool, stepping in before she did something memorable. "It's okay, Amber. We're just talking."

She turned on me, eyes fierce. "You sure? Because I'll throw his sorry ass into the bay if he even thinks about hurting you again."

"I'm sure. I just ... Need to hear him out."

Mitch nodded solemnly and focused on Amber. "Thank you for looking out for her when I failed to."

That gave her pause. Her expression didn't soften, but she backed off. Just barely.

"Shall we?" He asked, the crook of his arm twitching as if he wanted to offer it but wasn't sure if he should.

Instead, he guided me outside, where the coastal air kissed my cheeks. I felt the thrum of nerves low in my belly—nerves, and something else. Life. Four weeks of it. Quiet, steady. Real.

He hovered beside the car. "I didn't plan any of this. The cheating, the fallout, losing you. I don't know how to fix what I broke, but I'm desperate to try."

I hesitated before slipping into the passenger seat. "Drive."

He took us north, past the airport, silence

stretching thick between us. The further we got from town, the tighter my chest became, the more I questioned what I was doing.

When he finally pulled off at a little roadside café, something flickered in my memory—like a photo you can't quite place. He returned with two paper bags full of savoury, hot food and drove a little further before turning off into a wooded area by the coast.

The moment I stepped out, the smell of pine, sea salt, and something older than both hit me. My feet crunched along the gravel path. We walked in silence until we reached the picnic area, a tucked-away spot with views of the lighthouse and the horizon bleeding lavender and tangerine.

I sat slowly. "You brought me here for a reason. So talk."

"You know what's weird?" Mitch said softly, unpacking the containers. "I used to hate eggs."

I blinked, wondering where that conversation was leading. "What?"

"Couldn't stand the smell, the texture, nothing. Then you made them. Every weekend. And I started trying them, just to be polite. Turned out, I only hated them the way *I* made them." He looked at me. "That's how I feel about a lot of things now. I didn't realize how much I needed to change until you showed me better." He set a container in front of me and straightened his shoulders. "Five years ago, I did something unforgivable. I told myself it was a mistake, just one night. And I had to live with what it really was: a very poor choice. One I made without thinking of you."

"I still don't want to hear details."

"I need to say them." He didn't look away. "I met Jasmine for dinner in Campbell River. She was... vulnerable. Sad. I was two beers in and stupid, and she touched me, and instead of stopping her, I let myself disappear into the attention."

Pulling my focus off him, I stared at the waves. "You let her make you feel wanted."

"Yes." His voice cracked. "And I'm not proud of it. I came home early that trip and promised to devote myself to you, when you were ready. You were worth waiting for, even if it was years. I didn't want her—never did—I wanted you. I still do. That's never changed."

His words grabbed my attention and, finally, I looked at him, staring at the flash of trepidation in his eyes.

"And then I think about how much I—we—had. You. Our life. What we were building. I didn't picture a future because I thought what we had didn't need one. We were living in the present. Everything felt unshakable."

"But it wasn't."

"No. And I shook it. I shattered it."

He reached into one of the containers and used a

fork to carve my name into the Styrofoam lid. A ridiculous little heart around it. "You were always the one. Even back then when I was being too dumb to admit it out loud."

I didn't reach for his hand. I didn't soften. Not yet.

"I thought I'd lost you for good. I woke up every morning hoping it was a nightmare. Every night, I wished I could go back and stop myself for having given in. To her."

I studied him—really studied him. His hands shook. His shoulders were tight, drawn in. There was guilt there, but something else, too. Fear.

"Are you afraid you'll screw up again?"

"I'm human, of course I'm going to screw up, but what I'm terrified about the most is not being good enough for you. For the baby." His gaze dropped briefly to my stomach before returning to lock on my eyes.

There it was—raw, unvarnished. No charm. Just a man stripped down to the bone.

"You didn't even want Jackson," I said quietly. My hands instinctively covered my belly.

"I didn't expect him. That's different. Had she not needed to move stateside, it's quite likely I would've never learned about him." He tucked his chin in and his gaze fell to the table. Inhaling a deep breath, he lifted his head. "I don't deserve to be a father, and I know I'll never be perfect, Cedar, but I want to try. With him. And especially with ours." His chest expanded with a deep breath. "If you'll let me."

My breath caught in my throat and I forced myself to choke out the words. "But you are one. That's not a choice anymore." I sat back. The food went cold in front of me. "Doubt has infiltrated our relationship, and I find it hard to trust you."

"I wouldn't expect you to." He swallowed hard. "But I'll work as hard as I can to rebuild that, for as long as it takes. Prove myself. Every day."

I nodded and rose, unable to eat.

We walked then, letting the wind carry away what neither of us could say. I kept a step ahead, needing the space. Needing air. When we reached the lighthouse, five-year-old memories collided—his mouth on mine, the first flush of falling, the way he'd held me like I was something sacred. It was then I had committed to him. To us.

The light circled around a few times as I revelled in the mental flashbacks. After Mitch kissed me, something changed inside—I knew in my soul he was the one for me. Up until a week ago, there had never been any doubt.

A glowing ember of hope ignited. "Until then, until I believe in you and me again, what happens to us?"

"I guess the first question would be finding out if you'll ever forgive me? Some day."

Tough question, with an answer I wasn't sure about. "I don't know. I really don't."

Feeling his hurt, I put a little distance between us and walked closer to the edge of the water, focused on the spray shooting into the air as the waves crashed harder against the rocky escarpment.

His feet crunched over the gravel as he approached but kept a safe distance. "I know I said before how I was just comfortable being us. But I've changed my opinion." His sweet smile was ribboned with sadness, and I couldn't bear to look in his direction. "People change, and I'll be the first to admit, it happened to me. Because of you."

Would he change? Would he be okay with being a father – a full-time father? Because that was what I wanted more than anything, even though I was willing to do it alone, especially after seeing how quickly he dismissed Jackson.

The escarpment blurred as I listened to his breathing and tried to imagine a life—a future—where Mitch wasn't in it. And it was heartbreaking.

Mitch cleared his throat. "You once asked what the future looks like. I don't have a perfect answer. But I want you in it. Our child. Whatever comes our way, I'm here. I always have been. Cedar, I love you with everything I am, and I am so sorry I hurt you and for the rest of my life, I will never forget that and will work hard to earn back your trust."

With a trembling heart, I faced him.

He tipped his head to the side, covering his heart with his hand. "I want to be part of this. Even if you hate me. Even if you never look at me the way you used to." A pained smile ghosted across his face.

Slowly, he lowered himself onto bended knee and reached into his coat, pulling out a ring box.

My stomach clenched.

"Don't," I said. "Not like this."

He froze mid-lift.

"You don't get to just rewrite the past with a ring and a sunset."

The box stayed in his hand. Unopened. He looked like he'd just realized it wasn't a fairytale anymore.

"I know," he said. "I'm not trying to fix this with a proposal. But I had one planned—before everything fell apart. It was supposed to be our anniversary surprise. I had it all worked out."

My heart stuttered.

"Cedar Ratzloff, you're the only person who's ever known me fully and still chosen me. Even when I didn't deserve it. I want to be the kind of man you can depend on. Not because I'm perfect—but because I'll fight like hell to love you right. Every day. Will you marry me? Someday?" He lifted the lid of the box.

Silence.

The waves beat the rocks. The lighthouse turned.

I blinked, heart thundering.

Could I believe everything he was saying? Or was this just nostalgia wearing a diamond ring?

My feet were rooted to the ground and my breath froze in my lungs.

"I've always loved you, Cedar. It's always been you I've wanted. If nothing else, I need you to believe that."

I inhaled sharply, my gaze dropping to the ring and back up to his eyes. Yes, in all the time we've been together, he's been my man. I never had any doubts. Not a single reservation. Until she dropped the bomb.

My breaths were long and steady. I rolled my bottom lip between my teeth as I studied his face and all the sincerity he wore. Finally, I exhaled a weighted sigh.

"I want you there," I said softly. "For the midnight feedings. The midwife visits. The good. The rough. All of it. I'm not doing this halfway."

"I wouldn't ask you to."

I pressed a hand to my belly, as tears escaped their hold. "I'm saying yes—not because it's easy, but because I believe people can change. Because I still love you. But you don't get to coast, Mitch. Not ever again."

He didn't grin. He looked like a man who'd just been handed grace he didn't think he'd earned.

"I love you," he whispered.

"I know. Now prove it."

He stood, slipped the ring onto my finger, and pulled me close. His kiss wasn't triumphant—it was trembling, reverent.

After a long moment, I pulled back, breathing in a rare, quiet peace.

He pressed his forehead to mine. "I'll never take you for granted. I swear."

And for the first time since that flight landed, I believed him.

We stood there—two people with scar tissue, wind at our backs, a baby between us and the future stretching like the horizon.

Love wasn't a fairytale. Maybe it was this: the choice to stay, to try, to believe again.

Even when it hurt.

Especially when it mattered.

"Is there anything else from your past I should know about?"

Mitch swallowed hard. "Nothing like what I already told you. Nothing that would change how I feel about you. But I'm sure there are things I didn't notice back then—ways I failed you I didn't even realize. I'm still learning how to see them." He hesitated. "But... there is one thing."

I braced.

"There's a cedar tree near the spot of our first kiss.

Carved our initials into it five years ago. Dumb thing, but... I guess I wanted something permanent. Just in case I messed everything else up."

I blinked at him. "You did mess everything else up."

He gave a sad little smile. "And yet the tree's still there."

"And so are you." I swallowed. "And so am I."

"I love you, Cedar."

"And I love you, Mitch. Always have and always will."

Epilogue

A few weeks later, I was sitting at my desk, flipping
through a pregnancy magazine when the walkie-
talkie cackled from the tower.

"We have an inbound Aerostar on emergency
approach. Clear the runway and prep for landing."

I grabbed the walkie-talkie and scrambled over to
the bank of windows, pushing out onto the tarmac. Where
was Mitch? Surely, he heard.

Eric came out of the bay and flagged me over,
radio in hand.

"What's the 911 for?"

He scanned the skies. "Forced landing. Lost
power."

"That's not good. How big is an Aerostar?" Not
the size of a jumbo jet, I hoped.

Our airport wasn't built to handle the big planes,
mostly just the ones with a ten-seat max kind of deal. Like

the private jets.

"She's slightly bigger than my plane."

"We'll have enough runway?"

Eric shrugged, still scanning the sky for the inbound plane. "Depends on how far out she lost power. If she slowed enough, then we should be okay. However, they chose our airport because if she's coming in hot and too fast, they'll have to ditch in the ocean."

An open body of the bay lay beyond the end of the runway, probably why the airport was built here – to facilitate those types of landings in a worse case scenario.

"Where are they coming from?"

"Tower, this is Captain Eric Morris. What's the ETA and original destination?"

"Three minutes." The radio crackled. "Inbound from Masset Muni heading to Tacoma. Two crew, one passenger."

"Roger."

Whoever they were, they'd left the Queen Charlotte Islands and were heading into the USA.

Mitch exited the building and walked over to me, wiping his hands on a wipe. "Mechanical?" His question geared to Eric.

"We'll see."

"We have visual." The tower radioed over.

"Incoming." Eric pointed, and I followed his finger to the general direction.

The plane was indeed coming in hot and fast.

"Get inside," Mitch said, and pushed me toward the door.

But I couldn't leave. Instead, my eyes locked onto the plane barely sailing above the treetops.

"They're going to belly land on the end of the runway." Eric's voice pitched. "There's no landing gear."

"You're going inside." Mitch picked me up and carried me in, Eric right on his heels.

I didn't need to know when the plane was close, the grating metal against asphalt was a sound not to be missed. I cringed and covered my ears to the scraping. It didn't take long, because the plane was going so fast, but it skidded by the main building in a heartbeat, and we plastered ourselves against the windows to watch as it headed towards the sea.

Since the immediate danger had passed, we stepped outside and continued to watch. The airport firetruck lit up and was ready to go. The local ambulance drove behind the building and idled, waiting for a go.

After another few heartbeats, the plane finally stopped moving. Eric and Mitch ran over and hopped into the ground's vehicle, driving straight to the crash site. From my point of view, everything looked okay – at least it wasn't a crash-crash and there wasn't debris scattered everywhere. It was going to be an expensive bill to fix the plane though.

In what felt like forever, the radio crackled with a no personal injury report on all three onboard from Mitch. Sweet relief, that was great news.

I set about calling the nearest motels to find lodgings, and since we were approaching the Canadian Thanksgiving weekend, there were only a few available. I scratched down the information for the new guests to the area.

Some time later, Eric pulled up in the vehicle, and two men and a woman got out.

"Greetings, and welcome to Cheshire Bay." I approached the Captain first.

"Thank you," he said. "I'm Captain Elijah Lancaster. This is my first officer, Miss Sorcha Browne, and our passenger, Mr. Welsh." There was a lilting accent; Irish perhaps? Maybe European?

Mr. Welsh, whose first name was a guess, seemed a person of importance, as the two crew members flanked either side. Plus, he was a trifecta of swoon. Tall, dark-haired, and incredibly handsome.

I shook all their hands and cleared my throat, reminding myself the necessity of being an ambassador to Cheshire Bay and to the airport.

"Is everyone okay?" I quickly scanned their persons, no one seemed hurt, and they all walked without the telltale sign of limps from broken bones or sprains. "Shall I call the EMTs?"

"We are all fine. Checked us out as we de-boarded."

Quickly, I did another roving assessment. Indeed, no one seemed physically hurt, but I imagined the emotional trauma was hidden.

"I suspect you will require lodgings while you wait for another flight or repairs." Since this had never happened at my airport, I wasn't sure the right protocols and my brief training on the subject escaped my brain. "I've spoken with a couple of motels, and these are the top three I'd recommend."

The available rooms were no Marriots or Hiltons, but they had the best views of the ocean which helped bump their 2.8 stars closer to 3. One in Cheshire Bay, and two in Stewart Surf.

"Thank you." The pilot took my list, gave it a once over and handed it to Mr. Welsh. "This is most helpful."

"I really need a drink." The tall one spoke in a different accent I couldn't place. It certainly wasn't local. It wasn't even Canadian.

I quickly searched his hand and there was no ring. Was he single? Maybe.

Cupid sat above my shoulder and readied his arrow.

"There's a great local pub in Cheshire Bay and the owner is the absolute best in the business." I grabbed a pad of paper from my desk and scratched down the name and address of the place. "Ask for Amber."

Mr. Welsh took the information and folded it up, sticking it into his shirt pocket. He turned his back to me and whispered to the crew, maintaining his rigid posture. Finally, he spun on the heel of an expensive shiny shoe, removed his sunglasses, and spoke in broken English. "Would it trouble you, please call taxi service?"

Where was this foreign chap from?

Since I was finished my shift for the day and had nothing better to do than see the look on Amber's face when he walked into her bar, I volunteered. "I'll do you one better. Amber's Ale isn't too far away, I'll drive you over."

"Your hospitality be appreciated."

"Actually," Eric walked over, giving me a what-the-hell-are-you-thinking look. "I'll take you there. I'm sure Cedar has a ton of paperwork to pull up."

Not really, but I understood what he was doing, the sweet guy he was. Eric probably had paperwork of his own to fill out, witness statements and all that jazz.

"Give me five minutes," Eric said to Mr. Welsh, dashing over to another desk to make a quick phone call.

"Thanks, Eric."

Besides, Mitch probably would've lost his mind had I escorted a stranger somewhere, even if nothing truly exciting ever happened in this part of the world. This crash landing would be gossip for months.

Mr. Welsh stood there, hands clasped behind his back while speaking in clipped foreign words to the pilot and captain. His pilot tapped him on the arm when Eric hopped back over.

"Alright. Let's go. Right this way."

"Remember, ask for Amber." I waved as Eric and Mr. Welsh stepped back onto the tarmac and disappeared under the watchful eyes of the flight crew. "Can I get you anything? Is there anyone I can call for you?"

They pulled out their phones, as the pilot opened the door and stepped outside. "We're good for now." Her voice had a lilting accent as well, but nowhere near as strong as Mr. Welsh's.

"Just holler if you need anything." In the meantime, I had a quick call to place myself. I dialled my friend.

"Hey, what's up?"

"Nothing much." I twirled the phone cord, making jump rope movements. "You have a VIP coming in who'll be asking specifically for you. His plane just belly landed here, and he needs a stiff drink."

I wanted to drop hints about the melodic accent or the dashing good looks that come from amazing genes. Assuming he wasn't married, he'd be good for keeping Amber entertained for a couple of hours, if she gave him the time of day. However, she'd always been a sucker for an accent.

"Thanks for the heads up. I gotta run."

"Have fun." A smile beamed out of me like a ray of sunshine.

The Cheshire Bay Series

DREAMERS in CHESHIRE BAY

Cheshire Bay's resident ambassador is ready to declare war, not fall in love.

RETURN to CHESHIRE BAY

It's hard to start over, and find love, when no one forgets your past.

ADRIFT in CHESHIRE BAY

She's ready to surprise her boyfriend. Turns out she's going to be the one in shock.

AWAKE in CHESHIRE BAY

An emergency landing, a sexy stranger, and a night she's never going to forget.

CHRISTMAS IN CHESHIRE BAY

Can a Christmas miracle happen even if you don't believe in the magic?

JOURNEY to CHESHIRE BAY

A homeless dropout with nothing to live for. A socially inept astrophysicist with a detailed future. A cross-country journey that will forever alter their lives.

CHARMED IN CHESHIRE BAY

No kissing, no dating, and no matter what, absolutely no falling in love.

SECOND CHANCES IN CHESHIRE BAY

Thirteen years apart. Two shattered hearts beyond repair. One shot at a second chance neither of them saw coming.

UNFORGIVEN IN CHESHIRE BAY

Revenge is never a fool-proof plan.

FLIRTY IN CHESHIRE BAY

An estranged sister, a flirtatious connection, and the one thing she never thought she'd lose – her heart.

More Fabulous Reads

Dear Reader

The Cheshire Bay series has been one of the most fun series I've written. I've enjoyed spending my time there, and drawing up the maps, creating the family trees, and picturing the completely fictional town. Why can't Cheshire Bay be real?

Keep reading the series and learn more about Lily, Cedar, Amber, Mona, Iris, Summer, Chloe, Erin and Libby and their personal journeys to growth and love.

Would you like to be the first to know of upcoming releases, see the covers before anyone else, and just have all the insider information? Then you'll want to join my twice-a-month mailing list. Connect through my website – www.hmshander.com. I promise not to spam you, and I keep things fun with freebies and a scavenger hunt. Your time is valuable, and I appreciate how you've spent time reading my story (thank you for that!).

Finally, if you don't mind, I'd love a review on your favourite retailer site for Return to Cheshire Bay. It doesn't have to be long, even just as simple as "Mitch is my new book boyfriend" works. Reviews and ratings help me gain visibility, and as I'm sure you can tell, reviews are tough to come by. Thank you so much for spending time with me.

Yours,

H.M. Shander

acknowledgements

If one good thing came out of the pandemic in 2020, it was these books – I'm absolutely in love with this series and all the characters. They are each unique, but together, they form a beautiful series, if I do say so myself.

I'm in awe of being able to do what I love, and to fulfill my dream, but writing these thanks yous never gets easier. Never. Always afraid I'll miss someone, or a category will be left out. And then I wonder, does anyone even read these? I know as an author, I do, but I wonder if readers do? Anyways, writing a book for the most part, is a solo endeavor, but I could not have this ready for you to read if not for the cheerleading and support of some magnificent people in my life.

First – my Shander family, whom you may know on my social media platforms as Hubs, The Teen, and Little Dude. Thank you from the bottom of my heart for letting me pursue what I love doing, for something that allows me to transport myself to another time and place – the summer of 2020 was a particular straining time, and you gave me this golden escape into the pages. For that, I'll be forever grateful, and if this series does well, we're going to do something incredible. Like really big and fun. Thank you for cheerleading as I had a sale, and watching the numbers climb. Thank you for encouraging me to keep going and to chase my dreams, and for the nonstop coffees I sometimes needed when I was on a role. I love you all with my whole heart.

To my parents and in-laws and extended family – Thank you for your support and encouraging your friends and family to give my books a try. Having you visit me at markets and book signings means the world. I have an amazing family, and every day I'm thankful to you all. Thanks for being you.

To my wonderfully dedicated alpha reader – Mandy. My trusted go-to writing pal, the one who reads the first cleaned up draft. Where would I be without your support and guidance? Probably still cowering in a corner. Your comments and feedback are vital to me. I never have to wait long, and before I know it, my inbox has a response, and 99% of the time, your advice is bang on. I'm so glad we're in this business together, and you know I'm your biggest fan and cheerleader! You're going to go big, and I'm tagging along on the ride. You deserve the very best.

To my critique partner – Josephine. Thank you for spending your free time reading my words and pointing out what didn't make sense and what needed to be expanded on. How many times did I redo that opening chapter in Return? LOL, and Awake? You had your work cut out with that, eh? But, as always, your insight was invaluable, and the stories are better with your touch! Thank you.

To my beta readers – Shauna, Melissa, and Dawn. Thank you for cheering for the good, highlighting the bad, and letting me know what worked and what needed more explanation. Your feedback and insight are a gift I cherish.

To my cover designer – Eleanor. Great job! I'm super thrilled with how well all the covers turned out, including the special edition print cover! I simple adore all of them and can't stop staring! I'm so blessed to have discovered your talents, and I look forward to many more covers designed by you.

To my editor – Irina. Thanks for your dedication to fixing my errors and highlighting the inconsistencies. I think I'm getting better, right? At least it's not the same corrections every time. Heh-heh.

If I missed you, it certainly wasn't intentional. I know I couldn't be where I am without the help of so many others. Thank you! And thank you for reading and making it all the way to the end. You all rock.

about the author

USA TODAY bestselling author H.M. Shander is a star-gazing, romantic at heart who once attended Space Camp and wanted to pilot the space shuttle, not just any STS – specifically Columbia. However, the only shuttle she operates in her real world is the #momtaxi; a reliable electric car that transports her two kids to school and various sporting events. When she's not commandeering Elektra, you can find the elementary school librarian surrounded by classes of children as she reads the best storybooks in multiple voices. After she's tucked her endearing kids into bed and kissed her trophy husband goodnight, she moonlights as a contemporary romance novelist; the writer of sassy heroines and sweet, swoon-worthy heroes who find love in the darkest of places.

If you want to know when her next heart-filled journey is coming out, you can follow her on Instagram (@HMShander) or Facebook (hmshanderauthor).

Thanks for reading– all the way to the very end.

www.ingramcontent.com/pod-product-compliance
Lightning Source LLC
Chambersburg PA
CBHW050829180626
46814CB00004B/1530